Wylder Bachelor

by

Virginia Barlow

The Wylder West

Wylder Bachelor

Cover Art by *The Wild Rose Press, Inc.*

The Wild Rose Press, Inc.
PO Box 708
Adams Basin, NY 14410-0708
Visit us at www.thewildrosepress.com

Publishing History
First Edition, 2021
Trade Paperback ISBN 978-1-5092-3842-2
Digital ISBN 978-1-5092-3843-9

The Wylder West
Published in the United States of America

"There's nothing to worry about. A stranger came in asking questions. He's gone now. No one knows you're here."

"Who is he? What did he want?" Miss Jones licked her lips. She must be thirsty again.

He poured her another glass of water.

She lifted herself up to take the glass. Jackson slid behind her and helped her until she pushed it away. Strangers must frighten her. Miss Jones trembled like an autumn leaf in the breeze.

He laid her back against the pillow. "Mr. Smythe asked about a gunshot cowboy. I sent him to Doc Sullivan."

Miss Jones stiffened and paled a bit more. "Mr. Smythe?"

"I won't let anyone hurt you," he said. "Do you want to tell me what happened?"

Miss Jones lifted tortured eyes to his. "I did. My father wants me to marry a horrible man. I…ran away…and got involved in something I shouldn't. I got shot in the process." Her big blue eyes looked up at him. She swallowed a sob. "I can't go back. Please don't make me."

"I might run a livery, but I am a gentleman." One wouldn't know it by the thoughts going through his head every time he looked at her. Jackson kept his gaze on her face. He didn't want her to notice he knew the front of her nightgown came unbuttoned while she slept. He didn't want her to know how sexy he thought she was with her hair messed up and a blush on her cheeks. Jackson stared at her mouth. He shouldn't think about kissing her soft lips, either. He cleared his throat. "I brought you some dinner."

Dedication

For Roy John and Rulon.
You will always have a place in my heart.

Chapter One

Lonetree, Wyoming Territory
June 1880

There was one thing left to do.

Take from Phineas Wagner the thing which meant more to him than she did—his money.

Maryanne Lucy Wagner tugged the borrowed breeches over her backside and fumbled with the buttons down the front. How did men get in and out of the things anyway? She buttoned the waist and let go. The breeches slipped to her hips. One of the problems with being a girl? Her hips were wider than her waist. Maryanne frowned at her reflection. She would need suspenders to keep the breeches up. She couldn't rob the bank and make a decent getaway if one hand kept her pants on. She grabbed Papa's newest pair from the oversized bed in her room and fastened them to her waistband. The white and gold braiding gleamed in the candlelight.

Papa bought the suspenders on his last business trip to New York. The trip he signed her life away. Anger thinned her lips. At nineteen, she should have a say in who she didn't want to marry. And William Smythe occupied number one on the list. If anyone bothered to ask her, she would have told them she didn't want to get married at all. She would have been born a boy. As a man, she could come and go whenever she pleased, say what she wanted, do what she wanted, pick her own marriage partner, and decide her own fate. As a woman, she had none of those choices. Maryanne hadn't found one good thing yet about being a girl.

Which brought her back to Papa. His bank, Wagner Trust, was in trouble. Papa needed money. A few unfortunate investments, and Maryanne learned what she always suspected. Papa loved his bank and his money more than he loved her. A longtime acquaintance, Bernard Smythe, president of Smythe Bank and Trust of New York City, offered to keep Wagner Trust in business. Papa signed the legal papers last time he went to New York. The day he bought the suspenders.

Bernard and Papa were friends most of their lives. When Bernard learned Wagner Trust teetered on bankruptcy, he hot footed it to Wyoming Territory to make an offer. Maryanne's hand in marriage to his son William in exchange for the money to keep Wagner Trust in business. Papa took the train to New York to meet with the Smythe Bank and Trust lawyers and solidified the deal within the week Maryanne shivered. Bernard Smythe grew weary of bailing William out of trouble. He saw an opportunity to make William respectable after all his scrapes with the law, and he took it. At Maryanne's expense.

Her engagement to William Smythe equated to indentured servitude. Bernard believed women should know their place. His son shared the same views, with a sadistic twist. William beat women into submission. Maryanne had no intention of being anyone's slave.

Resentment tightened her chest. She wore Papa's

new suspenders in rebellion against the situation.

He would be furious when he woke up tomorrow and realized his money vanished. Visions of him walking into an empty bank lightened her mood. She pictured the surprised look on his wrinkled face and laughed. He would be livid.

Maryanne doubted he would notice her disappearance until he needed an errand run. She tugged the long sleeve flannel shirt on and buttoned it up. As she tucked the shirt into the baggy breeches and stretched the expensive suspenders over her shoulders, her smile widened. In a few hours, she would be on her way to a new life. A life without William Smythe, a life without Lonetree, and a life without Wagner Trust. Maryanne tugged on her boots. She would be on her own and make her own choices. The possibilities were endless.

Once she dressed, Maryanne plaited her long blonde hair and pinned it to her head in a large coil. She covered it with a man's hat. She borrowed that the same time she took the breeches and shirt.

Maryanne twirled around and high-stepped in place. She marveled at the freedom. The men's breeches were light as air. Riding a horse would be so much more fun.

Maryanne peeked out her bedroom window. The barns and orchards behind the house were outlined by the silver light of the full moon. She planned this night for weeks.

Maryanne apologized in her head to whatever cowboy owned her outfit. He lost a set of clothes while she gained her freedom. It didn't seem fair, but then life never was.

The Lazy J ranch fell behind in their payments to the bank. Phineas Wagner sent Maryanne to speak to Hank Jessup, owner of the Lazy J. She went in the middle of the day when she knew all the hands would be out fixing the fence. She didn't go to the main house. She visited the bunkhouse instead. Once she collected what she wanted from the hand's saddlebags, she high tailed it back to town. It would be a couple of weeks before Papa discovered she had not delivered his message about the payment. By then, she planned to be in California or on a boat to the Orient. Anywhere but here.

Maryanne stared at her reflection in the mirror. The candlelight danced across her face. She tugged the hat forward to hide more of her face. She slid Papa's pistol into the front pocket of her breeches and cinched the suspenders tighter. She grabbed her packed valise from the bed and replaced it with a note addressed to her father. Maryanne informed him she would be in Omaha at her mother's younger sister, Ethel's house, for several weeks. She lied to cover her tracks. Ethel died of consumption last year, but Phineas Wagner never listened to her. His lack of attention gave her the advantage.

The note gave her time to make a getaway without drawing the town's suspicions. If anyone asked, Papa would say she went to Omaha.

Maryanne glanced around the room. Time to go. She blew out her candle and slipped out of the house. Maryanne considered using her own mare but changed her mind. She didn't want Papa or any of the townsfolk to connect her to the robbery.

She climbed onto her stolen mare and hooked her

valise on the saddle horn.

Papa owned a fine two-story wooden house at the end of Main Street, several lots down from the Whiskey Barrel Saloon. Maryanne stole the mare from the hitching post outside the saloon and led her home through the back streets as soon as the mare's owner disappeared behind the swinging doors. Most of the men who came on Friday nights stayed for hours.

She figured if the owner discovered his mare missing, she would hear the commotion and release the horse. Then she would wait for another cowboy looking for drink and women and take his horse. The saloon did a lot of business on Friday and Saturday nights, so she had options. Maryanne hid the mare in the stable at home until Papa fell asleep. He went to bed every night at eight. So, she had a couple of hours to wait, and the cowboy should be busy in the saloon at least that long.

Maryanne stayed in the shadows as she made her way to the back of the bank. It stood between the General Store and the barbershop. The feed store resided between them and the saloon. She tied the horse to a post inside the little stable out back.

The Whiskey Barrel Saloon filled with customers. Music and laughter floated on the night air. Maryanne looked around. The area behind the bank was deserted.

Papa knew she did not want to marry William, but he didn't care. "Women should tend to women things and leave the thinking to the men," he said when she tried to explain why. He used his fists when she argued. After a while, she gave up trying to make him understand. William possessed a twisted, evil mind and unusual appetites. When Maryanne brought up several incidents William had been involved with, Papa waved them away with the same dumb explanations Bernard used to excuse his son's behavior. The police never convicted William or arrested him for any of the crimes he committed. Women were beaten and abused, and William walked around free. The witnesses accepted bribes, or they disappeared. As a result, William grew arrogant and reckless. The things he used to do in secret, he now did in the open.

The music stopped, and another riotous song began. The heavy chords rang through the warm night air. Crickets chirped nearby. The scent of stale hay, sagebrush, and horse manure assaulted her nostrils. Maryanne tiptoed across the bright moonlit ground to the back door of the bank and picked the lock. The door swung in, and she stepped into Papa's office. The moonlight lit the room through the open door. She hurried to the safe. She could be shot for robbing the bank, but she didn't care. Papa wouldn't listen to her. Nobody listened to her. She would never be William's wife. She would never be anyone's wife. Marrying a sadistic fiend wasn't her idea of happiness.

Maryanne spun the dial on the safe. She found Papa's diary in his desk at home and memorized the combination. She could just make out the numbers and worked the dial back and forth. Once the safe swung open, Maryanne pulled out all the bills and packed them in her saddlebags. She added all the gold and silver coins. Then she picked up the iron bar she brought with her and smashed the edges and side of the safe as if someone pried it open. She hid the bar in the barn and covered it with straw.

Maryanne lugged the saddlebags to her borrowed horse and secured them. Then she closed the back door of the bank and brushed her tracks away.

Mighty pleased with her success, she rounded the corner and caught sight of William's best friend, Rex Conway, standing on the wooden boardwalk in front of the saloon. One of the new whores in town stood beside him with her arms folded over her buxom chest. She had red hair and answered to Sadie.

Maryanne pulled her horse to a stop. Her route to freedom and a new life lay two hundred feet away, and now this. She turned and rode behind the barbershop. Maryanne guided her horse behind the buildings and walked the mare up the alley between the feed store and the saloon. Rex and Sadie stood on the boardwalk in front of her. It was dangerous to be this close. Someone might recognize her, or the mare's owner could stumble out and she'd be done for.

The mare side-stepped. Maryanne patted her neck to soothe her and bit her lip. Rex would recognize her if he saw her face. She tipped her hat forward and thought hard about what she wanted to do next.

Rex was as sadistic and twisted as William. Maryanne made sure they were never alone in the same room. Her gut told her he'd rape her if he got a chance, despite her betrothal to William.

"Leave me alone!" Sadie's shrill voice sliced through the night air. She sounded scared to death.

Maryanne lifted her head just enough to see the two of them. Rex had his back to her. His hands were on Sadie's arms.

"I paid good money for you. Now do what I say," Rex said. The meanness in his voice sent shivers down Maryanne's spine.

"I'm not going with you. I know what you did to

the other girls, and I'm not going." Sadie hit his hands away and turned to go.

Rex caught her arm and jerked her toward him. "I say you are. I have a little surprise for you at the cabin. I paid Miss Gwen extra to have you for the entire night. Now get your ass on my horse before I lose my temper." His voice turned silky soft.

Maryanne's breath caught in her throat. She knew what they did at the cabin. The girls who went out there came back bruised and broken. It took days before they could function again. Two of them never came back at all. William and his friends all took a turn. They had different tastes and played out their sick fantasies. Maryanne did not understand it at all. Why would a man enjoy hurting a woman? She shook her head. Whatever William and Rex had in mind for Sadie, it couldn't be good.

Maryanne overheard William and his friends one-night last week. Maryanne snuck into town to plan the robbery. As she came up the alley by the saloon in the dark, she heard William's voice and froze. He and his friends bragged about the things they did to the whores. They had a cabin a few miles outside of town. They took the girls there and used them. Maryanne listened for a few minutes hoping they would move on so she could get the distance measurement she came for. They didn't. After five minutes of their boasting, Maryanne turned to go. Bile rose in her throat over the things they said, and she lost her dinner behind the bank.

Maryanne wondered why Miss Gwen agreed to let Sadie go. She frowned. Unless Miss Gwen didn't know, and Rex lied to get his way.

Dammit! Maryanne frowned. She didn't care much

for the saloon girls, but she couldn't walk away and let Rex hurt Sadie either. Maryanne robbed the bank to escape what Sadie now faced.

Maryanne considered her options. She couldn't afford to let anyone see her. It would ruin her plan and her life. She kept her head down. Indecision furrowed her brow. Should she cause a scene and give Sadie a chance to get away? Maryanne looked toward the deserted street. She could start a fire in the woodpile and ring the fire bell. The men in the saloon would come pouring out, and Sadie would have an opportunity to get away. Or she could shoot Rex and save the world a lot of misery.

Rex made the decision for her. He backhanded Sadie across the face. Sadie went down like a dead weight. So much for a rescue attempt. Maryanne tipped her hat forward when Rex picked Sadie up and slung her over his saddle. He climbed up behind her and rode out of town. Maryanne decided to follow and look for an opportunity to help.

She kept back far enough Rex wouldn't notice her, but close enough to keep an eye on them. About five miles out of town, Sadie must have awoken. Maryanne heard Rex yelling and Sadie screaming. She kicked her mare into a gallop. When she got close, Rex had Sadie on the ground next to his horse, beating her with both fists.

Maryanne didn't think. She shot.

Rex swayed and fell to his knees. Sadie scooted backward. Rex fell face-first into the dirt. Sadie screamed again. Her eyes were wide with fright, and blood dripped from her bruised face.

Maryanne rode up and slid to the ground. She held

the pistol tight in one hand and walked toward them.

"Please…don't shoot me," Sadie cried out.

Maryanne glanced at her. "I came to rescue you, not hurt you." She deepened her voice and hoped she sounded like a man.

She turned her attention to Rex. He didn't move. When she got close, she nudged Rex onto his back with her boot.

His eyes flickered. Blood pooled from the bullet wound in his back and soaked into the ground around him.

"What the hell?" Rex said. He put his hands down to push himself up but fell back. He stared up at her face. "You."

Maryanne swallowed and took a step back.

"William got himself a gal with fire. Wish I knew it sooner…" He coughed, and blood splattered everywhere. He died a few minutes later.

Maryanne sat back on her heels. Her hands shook so hard she dropped the pistol. She shot and killed a man in cold blood. The worst part about it? She shot him in the back. Cowards shot men in the back. Perspiration broke out on her forehead. She bent forward and threw up. She dry-heaved for several minutes, and her hat fell off in the process. When she finished, she sat back on the ground. So far, she robbed a bank, stole a horse, and killed a man, all before midnight.

A sob broke the silence. Maryanne looked up.

Sadie leaned against the side of Rex's horse, staring at her. "Miss Maryanne?" Her eyes widened in surprise. "What're you doing out here dressed like a man?"

Maryanne cleared her throat. Her hands trembled. Damn, Sadie recognized her. "You can't tell anyone we were here. They'll kill us both for this." She indicated Rex with her chin. "If anyone asks, say you don't know anything." She stared at Sadie. "If the town finds out what happened, I'll be hanged."

Sadie gaped at Rex on the ground. "They won't find out. You saved my life. He would have hurt me bad." She gazed at Maryanne. "Thank you," she whispered. "And don't you worry none. I won't tell anyone. I promise."

Maryanne nodded. Her promise would have to do. "Can you make it back to town on your own?"

Sadie nodded and rose to her feet. "I can ride his horse."

Maryanne got to her feet as well. "You'll have to go somewhere they won't find you. You'll need to leave tonight." She looked from Sadie to her saddlebags and back. Sadie had as much to lose as she did. "I have something for you." She hurried to her saddlebags and withdrew one hundred dollars. She handed it to Sadie. "Go back to town, gather your things and get as far away as you can. They'll come looking for Rex. When they find out what happened, they'll hunt you down and torture you until you tell them what happened. Then they'll kill you because you know too much." She looked at Rex's horse. "I wouldn't ride his horse into town if I were you. They'll backtrack it."

Sadie nodded. "I can ride him part way and let him go."

A horse whinnied in the distance. The thunder of hooves reverberated in the darkness behind them.

"Someone's coming. You should get going,"

Maryanne said. She walked toward her horse. "Stay away from William Smythe and his friends."

Sadie climbed into the saddle. "I will. I can't thank you enough. You don't know what he planned to do to me."

Maryanne turned to look at her. "I do know. It's why I followed. Now get out of here."

Sadie gave her a quizzical look and turned toward town.

Maryanne gazed after her for a minute and then turned west.

A horse appeared in the moonlight a few hundred feet away. It blocked her path to California and the boat ride to the Orient.

Damn! She would have to lose the rider before she could continue with her plan. Maryanne whipped her horse around and kicked it in the side. She rode hard toward town. The rider would find Rex's body in a matter of minutes. He would be William or one of his friends. No one else rode this trail late at night.

A roar came from the area behind her. The rider found the body. Maryanne kicked the mare again and leaned forward, flattening herself as much as possible.

A shot whizzed by her shoulder. Horse hooves drummed on the trail behind her. Maryanne realized she would never outride the rider, not with Papa's money weighing her down.

She turned and ran into the sagebrush. A creek bed lay a few hundred feet in front of her. She could ditch the stranger there. A hot pain burned her side. Maryanne cried out. She'd been shot. Dammit to hell! Now what? She couldn't get caught. Her life depended on her getting away.

She would never, ever agree to marry William. She would never be a slave to a man. Especially one who cut women for fun. William and his friends made her skin crawl. They deserved to be strung up.

Another fire burned her shoulder. Maryanne cried out and hit the creek bed at full gallop. She kicked the mare in the sides and ran down the dry bed for a few hundred feet. Then she crossed over onto her daddy's land. She knew it like the back of her hand and crisscrossed her trail time and again. All the while, her shoulder burned like hellfire. Her side grew sticky and wet. Blood stuck to her shirt and dripped down her leg. Maryanne shook her head to get rid of the dizziness. She needed medical attention and soon. The town of Wylder was close. If she followed the train tracks, they would lead her there. She didn't hear the rider behind her anymore. With a sigh of relief, Maryanne turned her horse west and galloped hard.

She found the train tracks shining like two silver lines in the dark and trotted alongside them. She planned to buy a train ticket to California in Wylder, anyway. Now she would be delayed until she got some medical help.

An hour later, Maryanne rode into Wylder and headed for the livery stable. There were so many horses coming and going; it would be impossible to trace her mare. Once outside the large wooden doors, she slid to the ground. Dizziness washed over her. Maryanne rested her head against the mare's side. "Thank you, girl," she whispered.

She opened the doors and led the mare into the livery. It was empty and dark except for the light of the full moon shining through the open doors. Maryanne undid the saddlebags and let them fall to the ground. She unhooked her valise and set it beside the saddlebags. Then she led the mare from the livery and slapped her on the rump. "Get for home!"

The horse took off at full gallop.

Maryanne closed the livery doors behind her and dragged the saddlebags to an empty stall. She didn't have much time, so she hid them in the hay. She turned to grab the small valise she packed and never made it. She blacked out face down and knew nothing more.

Chapter Two

He found her the next morning.

Chet Jackson Daniels owned the livery in Wylder. Three-quarters of it, anyway. He bought into the partnership between his dad and Buck Standish more than a year ago when he moved to Wylder. When his dad died a few months back, he inherited his dad's share, making him the majority owner.

In his early thirties, Jackson stood six foot three with dark brown hair and hazel eyes. Named after his dad, he went by Jackson to avoid confusion. A quiet, thoughtful man, he got up before the sun. Mornings were his time of day. Jackson loved the crisp clean air. He enjoyed watching the sun creep over the horizon with a hot cup of coffee in his hand. As the rays of the sun shot across the land, warming the earth with its heat, it brought the promise of a new beginning. Promises and new beginnings were something he needed more of. He came to Wylder to put his past behind him and move on with his life.

Jackson set his empty mug on his worktable and went to muck out the stalls. He ran a clean livery. He was short-handed at the minute and looking for hands to hire on. Jackson had two men who came in around seven. With the amount of business he had, he could use two more.

Jackson had fifteen to twenty horses he boarded at

any given time. There was plenty to do to make sure the animals all got water, feed, and exercise. Jackson had another ten horses out in the livery yard, and those animals needed care, too.

He finished the fourth stall and entered the fifth. He came up short. A boot protruded from the pile at his feet.

"What the hell?" he asked.

He pulled the boot, and a slim figure emerged from the pile of straw. Bloody straw, Jackson noted. The stranger turned out to be a skinny kid who looked about sixteen. Jackson crouched down beside the young man and shook his arm. "Hey, are you okay?"

He got no response. Jackson knelt and shook the youth again. The boy didn't move. He pressed a finger against the boy's neck. The faint flicker of a heartbeat told him the kid lived. Jackson pushed his hat back. The boy needed a bath. He had a dark smudge on his cheek where he slept in the dirt, and his clothes were caked with blood and dirt. Jackson eyed the blood in the straw. The kid had been here for a few hours judging by the size of the puddle. The boy's shirt stuck to his side and shoulder. Jackson frowned. Just what he needed; a gunshot wound to start his day right. He gazed at the boy. Who could shoot a kid? He didn't have whiskers. His cheeks were as smooth as a baby's behind. He didn't have muscle either. The boy's arms were too skinny, and he had the soft hands of a girl. The kid hadn't done a good day's work in his life, or he would have the callouses to prove it. Jackson sighed. He'd better see how bad the wound was before he made any decisions. If the kid could be moved, he would take him to Doc Sullivan.

Jackson unbuttoned the kid's shirt. He expected to see a skinny hairless chest. A set of pearl white breasts flattened with bindings caught his attention. Jackson dropped her shirt as if burned and stared at the unconscious figure. What the hell had he stumbled on to? What woman in her right mind would parade around in men's clothing? It was indecent. His gaze dropped to the puddle of blood. Whatever the reason, she needed help. He inspected the wound on her shoulder. The bullet must have struck bone. There was no exit wound. Jackson sat back on his heels. A woman lie on the ground in his stall, and she'd been shot. Twice.

He buttoned the top two buttons of the flannel shirt she wore in case someone walked in. He pulled the bottom of the shirt away from her side and grunted. The wound had dried blood and fibers of her shirt stuck to it. The bullet grazed her side. From the looks of the wounds, someone shot her from behind. Jackson frowned.

The girl came to. She went berserk, trying to get away from him. To her credit, she didn't scream. She just beat him with both hands. "Get your filthy rotten hands off me!" she yelled.

Her blows didn't hurt. She didn't have the strength to do much damage. "Shhhhh," he soothed. "I just wanted to see how bad you were hurt before I took you to the doctor."

The girl stilled. Her hat came off in the fray. Her blonde hair was braided and pinned tight to her head. She looked up at him with two of the bluest eyes he'd ever seen. "Please, no. I don't need a doctor. I'll be fine. I just need a minute to clear my head."

Jackson gazed at her. "You need more than a minute. I figure it'll take you a couple weeks, at least, to recover from your wounds."

She went rigid. Panic flashed across her expressive face. Her big blue eyes filled with tears. "If you take me to the doctor, he'll find me." Her hands shook as she pulled her shirt back over the bullet wound. "If he finds me…I'm dead."

She bowed her head and wiped her cheeks with the back of her hand. She looked young and alone.

Jackson frowned. "Hey now. Don't cry." He looked around, feeling awkward as all get out. What could he do to help her? He hated crying women. They preceded him in doing something he shouldn't. "Who's looking for you?" Maybe he should start with whoever wanted her dead.

"The man my father wants me to marry."

Jackson scratched his head as he mulled it over. He shouldn't get involved. "Do you have someone who can help you?"

The woman shook her head. "I'm an only child. My mother died in childbirth. My dad is forcing me to marry a monster, so I ran away. I don't want anyone to know where I am." Her face paled.

Jackson thought she would black out again and reached for her arms.

The girl jerked away from him. Her blue eyes widened with fear. She licked her lips and folded her arms over her chest.

"I'm not going to hurt you. I thought you were going to faint." He held his hands up, palms facing her. "See? They aren't filthy or rotten. I want to help." He dropped one toward her in a friendly gesture. "Maybe we should start with names. I'm Chet Jackson Daniels. My friends call me Jackson. I own the livery."

The girl touched his hand. "Maryanne… Jones."

His eyebrow rose. "Jones?"

Miss Jones lifted her chin in challenge. "It's a name. What's wrong with it?"

He noticed her hesitation before she said her last name. He'd bet his last horseshoe she lied to him. "Nothing. Jones is a good name."

Miss Jones sagged against the straw. Her eyelids flickered.

"Do you know who shot you?" He wanted to find out more before he stuck his neck out.

Miss Jones shook her head. "I came upon a group of men. When they heard me, they pulled out their guns. I got scared and rode the other way. They followed and shot me."

Jackson rose to his feet. He looked around the livery. In another few minutes customers would start wandering in. If Miss Jones didn't want to be seen, he had to move her. He didn't want to get tangled up with whatever mess she was in, but he couldn't turn his back. He never could resist a lady in trouble. After what happened last time, he'd sworn off being a knight in shining armor. The dragons were bitches to kill. Jackson hesitated. He could help her for a few days, but no longer.

"I have a spare room you can stay in if you want," he offered. Half of him hoped she would turn him down.

"You live here?" Miss Jones asked.

Jackson nodded. "My dad kept a set of rooms in the back of the livery. I have one empty. It's nothing fancy. Most of the folks who come into town stay at Culpepper's Boarding House or one of the hotels."

Miss Jones nodded. She grabbed the side of the stall to pull herself to her feet. She didn't make it. She would have fallen to the ground, but Jackson caught her in his arms. She weighed nothing at all. He frowned. No wonder she looked so peaked. She would have to turn sideways on a windy day to keep from being blown away. He carried her toward the back of the livery and kicked open the door to the spare room. The room he stayed in when he came to see his dad. Jackson laid her on the colorful patchwork quilt and pulled her boots off. He remembered her valise and went to get it.

He ran into Tom Walker, one of his hired hands, on his way back through the livery. Tom was a good lad. He had black hair and green eyes. The local girls all had a thing for him, but Tom was too shy to pay them much mind.

"Can you do the stalls?" Jackson asked. "I've got something I need to see to this morning."

"Sure thing," Tom replied, grabbing a pitchfork from the tool bin.

He could use three or four men like Tom, He was honest and a good worker.

Jackson found her valise. He turned to go and spotted the saddlebags. He picked them up and frowned over the weight. What did she have packed in there? He carried them to the back of the livery. He opened the door to his spare room. Miss Jones remained in the same position he left her in. He grimaced and stepped inside. He shut the door and bolted it behind him.

He set her saddlebags on the floor beside the bed and put the valise on the chair against the north wall.

Then he set about removing Miss Jones' clothes. She had on a pair of bloomers beneath the breeches. So she did know how to dress like a girl. He pulled back the quilt and laid her on the sheets. She had nothing on but her cotton bloomers and the binding. She was slim and all female. He wondered what she looked like in a dress with her hair done up fancy.

Jackson shook his head. What difference would it make? He was over females, especially ones in distress. Abigail O'Conner ruined him. He would never dash to a woman's defense again. Not without proper investigation of the circumstances. He covered Miss Jones with the quilt. Ladies in trouble were bad news. He should know by now. If he could picture Miss Jones as poison ivy or a cactus, he'd be better off.

Jackson returned a few minutes later with his medicine bag and boiling hot water. He treated the sick and injured horses in the livery, so he had supplies to deal with Miss Jones' gunshot wounds. He also had the expertise. Four years of medical schooling at Harvard Medical should be enough to remove a bullet and prevent infection.

He took a shot of whiskey to get himself in the mood. "Here's to you, Miss Abigail. Thank you for ruining my life. Without you, I wouldn't be here today." He took another shot of whiskey for good measure. Then he washed his hands and picked up his scalpel.

The train whistled and blew its horn. Jackson grimaced. It was eight o'clock already, and he had a lot to do today.

Three hours later, he tied the ends of the linen strips together around Miss Jones' tiny waist and laid her back. He checked the bandage on her shoulder. He did it. The bullet lay in the metal tray next to his arm, and Miss Jones would live.

"Promises of new beginnings," he said to himself. He stoked the fire in the room. It was warm outside for June, but Miss Jones was still in shock. She lost a lot of blood, but she would pull through. The bullet struck her shoulder blade in the back, and the other one grazed her side. The bullet came out clean, and nothing critical had been injured with either shot. He put fifteen stitches in her side.

Jackson washed his hands and cleaned up the mess in the room. On his way out, he glanced at Miss Jones, so pale and still. Her lashes fanned out across her thin cheeks. She looked like a lost little girl in need of someone to care for her. Jackson sighed. He shook his head to rid himself of the idea it should be him. No. He would never be that person. Not ever again. Not after Abigail.

****

Maryanne came to a little at a time. She opened her eyes and stared at the pale green walls all around her. Where was she, and how did she get here? Her eyelids dropped over her eyes. She had the darnedest time keeping them open. She blinked again. A stiff wooden chair stood against the wall. Her valise sat on the seat. Maryanne frowned. *Where were her saddlebags?* Panic flooded her. The fire crackled, and Maryanne jumped. In Wyoming, a fire always came in handy, no matter the season. With the weather so unpredictable, you never knew if you would need one or not.

Maryanne sat up. Agonizing pain burned her shoulder and side. She stilled. Who patched her up? Did

Mr. Daniels call the doctor like he threatened? Anxiety rose high in her chest. If he did, they'd come for her. Anyone could ask the doctor about a gunshot wound and find out she was here. Maryanne forced herself to calm down. She would leave as soon as her head quit spinning. She looked at the sun coming in the window. It was late afternoon.

She threw her covers back and realized she wore her own nightgown. Someone had undressed and dressed her. She shook with the effort to sit up. Dizziness spun the room around and around. Maryanne put her head down and fought the pain. She inched toward the edge of the bed and swung her legs off. They weighed a ton. She had to use both hands and swing one leg and then the other. Her shoulder hurt like hell. As she leaned over, she got a glimpse of the saddlebags on the floor and froze. Did Mr. Daniels know about the money? If he looked inside, he would.

The door opened, and he appeared. "What the hell are you doing?"

He stepped inside the room and closed the door behind him. Maryanne glanced at him and froze. She guessed he stood over six feet. Her gaze rose to his. He had the most incredible eyes. They flashed green and then gold. He had a straight nose and a square chin. His chest and arms bulged with muscle. He placed his hands on his narrow waist and waited for her answer. The man was perfect.

Maryanne ripped her gaze from his body. "I'm leaving," she managed to get out. Her swollen tongue refused to form the words she wanted to say. Her body shook like an autumn leaf in the wind.

She closed her eyes and swayed. The next thing

she knew, Mr. Daniels stood beside her. He lifted her legs carefully back onto the bed and laid her back. The warmth of his hands made her shiver. She was so cold. The sheen of perspiration covering her cooled quickly without the warmth of her blankets. Mr. Daniels leaned close. Maryanne ducked behind her hands. She waited for him to strike her like William did when she irritated him. Nothing happened.

He froze for a second and then tucked the blankets around her.

She caught a whiff of coffee, cedarwood, and leather. Mr. Daniels had a clean earthy scent that made her insides quiver. He smelled good. She frowned. She'd best get some distance between them. She knew what happened when she let William get too close. She gazed at him in trepidation with his face inches from hers. Maryanne stared at his full lips and licked hers. They were alone in the bedroom, and she had nothing on her nightdress. Would he try to force himself on her? William did once. She kicked him in the privates. He let her go, but not before he blackened her eye. Her breath hitched in her throat. Mr. Daniels was a stranger. Would he try to hurt her like William? She darted a glance at his face.

Mr. Daniel's hazel eyes gazed into hers with concern. He stayed silent for a moment or two.

"I'm going to tuck your bedclothes in. There's nothing to worry about." He slid his hand beneath the mattress and patted the blanket. "There, that should do it." He straightened and stepped back.

Maryanne bit her lip with apprehension.

Mr. Daniels tucked his hands into his pockets. "Your temperature is normal, and your color looks good." He studied her face. "You're not in the clear yet. It took me two hours to dig out the bullet and another hour to clean out your wounds and get you stitched up. You lost a lot of blood."

Maryanne blinked. What? Then she remembered their conversation. "*You* stitched me up?" She kept her gaze glued to him. When she realized Mr. Daniels planned to keep his distance, all the fight went out of her. She sighed, exhausted. Sleepiness weighed down her eyelids, making it difficult to see him.

"Yes, I did." He frowned. "I don't know where you think you're going, but you're staying right here until you're well. You aren't strong enough."

Maryanne tried to nod her head. She wasn't sure her head did what she told it to do. A train rumbled in the distance followed by a whistle. Her bed jiggled as the train rolled past. Maryanne fell into a dreamless sleep and knew no more.

Chapter Three

The next week went by in a blur. She remembered warm soup spooned into her mouth. She heard trains coming and going. Her bed vibrated every time one rumbled past. Someone slipped God-awful medicine into her mouth and told her to swallow. Warm, gentle hands wrapped her wounds several times. Twice, an unseen person pulled a clean nightdress over her head and guided her arms into the sleeves. Maryanne frowned. She felt her head and found her hair loose. Someone undid the braids and brushed her hair out. Mr. Daniels, she supposed. He had soothing, gentle hands. She remembered how large and warm they were. He was a kind man and very considerate. She never met anyone like him before.

Maryanne's eyes fluttered open. She stared at the same pale green. *Her saddlebags!* She scooted to the edge of the bed and looked over. Relief flooded her. They sat in the same position as before. Nobody touched them. She had to hide them before someone looked inside. It amazed her Mr. Daniels hadn't. William would have. News of the bank robbery in Lonetree must not have reached Wylder yet.

She pushed herself to a sitting position and waited. The dizziness lasted a few seconds, nothing more. Maryanne nodded her head in satisfaction. It shouldn't be too much longer before she healed enough to leave.

She scooted to the edge of the bed and slid off. It took her legs a moment to quit shaking. Maryanne held onto the bed and bent. She scooted the saddlebags as far under the bed as she could. The effort caused the dizziness to return. It took all her strength to make it back into bed. Trembling with the effort, Maryanne laid back with a sigh. She hadn't fallen like she thought she would.

When her head quit spinning, Maryanne took stock of her surroundings. Her valise sat on a wooden shelf beneath a row of pegs. Warmth and the smoky scent of burning spruce came from the fire crackling in the stone hearth. Her hairbrush sat on a small table beside the bed. The wooden stiff-backed chair stood beside it. The vase on the table beside her bed smelled of lavender and wildflowers. Maryanne took a deep breath. The pain in her side subsided. She smiled. Soon, she would be breathing in the scent of the ocean and freedom.

The door to her room opened. Mr. Daniels walked inside with a tray of food. "Miss Jones, you're awake. How are you feeling?"

Maryanne turned toward him. "Like I've been shot."

Mr. Daniels nodded. " That's understandable." He set a metal tray on the table beside the bed covered with a cute red-and-white checked napkin. The tray held a bowl of soup, half a sandwich, and an apple. The soup smelled rich and savory.

Maryanne's mouth watered.

Mr. Daniels chuckled. "Smells good, doesn't it? My stomach growled all the way over."

Maryanne tore her gaze from the crockery containing the hearty soup. "All the way over from where?"

"Vincent House Hotel on Wylder Street. They have a restaurant for the hotel guests. I take my lunch there."

Fear settled in her rumbling stomach. If he brought her food from the hotel, they knew Mr. Daniels had a guest. How much had he told them? "Do they know about me?" She gripped her hands together in her lap while she waited for his answer.

"No." Mr. Daniels grabbed the chair and swung it around so he could straddle it. "Look, I know you are frightened, and I know people are looking for you. Give me some credit. I wouldn't put you in jeopardy."

Maryanne gazed into his beautiful hazel eyes. They were as clear as a summer day. Her gut said he told the truth. She nodded. "Okay."

He studied her for a second. "I don't want to be involved in whatever trouble you're in, but I won't add to it either. If you want to keep your presence a secret, it's fine by me."

Silence filled the room as Maryanne ate her sandwich.

Mr. Daniels cleared his throat. "Word is there was a murder a few miles west of here. Someone shot the man in the back and left him." He shook his head. "I think it would be best if you stuck around a little longer, at least until the murderer is caught. Only a coward shoots a man in the back. It isn't right for a fellow to die that way. A man should get the chance to look into the eyes of his killer and defend himself."

Heat rose to her cheeks. She didn't know what to say. Maryanne dropped her gaze so he wouldn't see the guilt in her expression. "There are times a man deserves to be shot in the back." She hoped she sounded like a disinterested party, not the murderer.

Mr. Daniels's eyebrow rose. "Give me one example."

Maryanne shook her head. She couldn't explain. He might piece it together. How did she say the man beat a woman senseless and she stopped him by shooting him? He wouldn't understand anyway. He was a man. Rex deserved to die for what he did to his victims.

"Can't think of anything, huh? You're a decent, respectable woman, Miss Jones. Whoever shot the man wasn't. The murderer should be hunted down and strung up."

Maryanne swallowed. Sadie didn't feel that way. She bet his other victims wouldn't either.

"Things might get a little interesting once people hear about the reward."

Her head shot up. "What reward?"

Mr. Daniels dropped his chin to his arms folded on the back of the chair and studied her face. "The man came from a wealthy New York family. The sheriff said they put up a thousand-dollar reward to find out who killed their son. It's a big deal. They're sending a private detective, too."

Maryanne's eyes widened. She hadn't considered Rex's family and their money when she shot him. Her focus had been to stop Rex from killing Sadie. "When is the detective going to be here?"

"Next week. I expect he'll go to Lonetree and snoop around before he goes anywhere else." His gaze swept over her face and settled on her downcast eyes. "Why do you look so worried?"

"No reason," Maryanne lied.

He frowned. "Do you know Rex Conway?"

Maryanne swallowed again. She forced herself to take a deep breath. "Is that the man's name?"

"Yes." His gaze never left her. "I've been wondering if he rode with the group of men you saw. Except he didn't get away."

Maryanne lifted her gaze to his. She looked deep into his eyes and lied her butt off. "I wouldn't know. I was too busy trying to escape to pay much attention to anyone else."

"Okay. I believe you." He sat silent for a minute. "If it's not the dead man, what's got you so upset?"

Maryanne blinked. "All the extra people coming into town. I don't know who shot me or why. I don't want anyone to know where I am. What if I am spotted by someone and gunned down while you're out shoeing a horse or something?"

Mr. Daniels smiled. "First of all, you look a mite different than the boy I found in my stall. Second, I shoe the horses here. The blacksmith shop is on the west end of the livery. I won't be far. No one is going to bother you. All you need to worry about is getting better." He rose to his feet and spun the chair back to its original position. "Eat up. I'll be back in an hour or so to check in on you."

"Mr. Daniels," Maryanne said as he strolled toward the door.

He turned and waited for her to speak.

"Thank you for helping me and not telling the doctor or the sheriff." She gazed up at him.

He stopped with his hand on the door latch. "You're welcome." The door closed behind him.

Maryanne sighed a breath of relief. She hoped Mr.

Daniels never found out who killed Rex. She couldn't bear for him to look at her with the same cold expression on his face.

Maryanne sat up. She reached for the crockery bowl with the hearty soup. It tasted as good as it smelled. She ate every drop. It filled her stomach with its warmth. When she finished, she laid back down and covered herself with the pretty multicolor patchwork. Once she could walk without passing out, she would leave. If the Conway's sent a detective, they would soon figure it out. Then there was Sadie. She could blab everything, and it would be all over for Maryanne. The Conway's were wealthy, just like the Smythe's. They would never admit their precious son did anything wrong. Maryanne had no intention of being hanged for filth like Rex Conway.

****

Jackson caught himself thinking about Miss Jones. She was never far from his thoughts these days. Someone had been abusive. Someone close to her, like her father or her fiancé. Jackson studied her reactions to him with dismay. She cringed every time he got close. She ducked behind her hands when he leaned over to tuck her blankets around her. She jumped when he reached across her. Once, he picked up the poker to the fire. He turned to look at her with it still in his hands. Miss Jones cowered in the far corner of her bed, her face alight with apprehension. Someone hit her and often. Jackson made a point to be slow and deliberate. He told her what he planned to do before he did it. He had been helping her for over a week now. Today, for the first time, she didn't cringe or jerk away from him. What kind of man would hit a little thing like her?

Jackson shook his head. His grandmother raised him to be a gentleman, and hitting women was akin to shooting a man in the back or stealing a man's horse. Even card sharks and outlaws drew the line there. He didn't blame Maryanne for running away.

Something frightened her. Fear flashed in her eyes when he talked about the Conway's sending a detective. Did she know something? Maybe she knew who killed Rex Conway and was afraid they would kill her too. Who were the men she saw, and why did they fire their guns at her? Someone shot her from behind just like Rex Conway.

He remembered the way she looked when he left. Her blonde hair spilled over her pillow in soft golden waves. Light shone from her big blue eyes, and a smile tugged at her soft lips when she spotted him with the tray of food. Her smile stayed in his mind the rest of the day. He didn't know what made it different from any other woman's smile, but it was. His heart sped up when he handed her the food. It was ridiculous. His instincts told him she lied. He didn't know what she had to lie about. She hadn't lived long enough to have a past. Not like him. His lips twisted. After the fiasco in Boston, Jackson figured Wylder would be the best place for him. He would go west and make a new start. Promises and new beginnings were why he came to Wylder.

His father, Chet Daniels, welcomed him with open arms. He hadn't visited his dad since he started medical school.

"How long are you staying, son?" Chet asked, his warm brown eyes studying his only progeny.

Jackson shrugged. "As long as you'll have me."

Chet Daniels sat his mug of coffee on the breakfast table. "What about all your medical schooling?"

Jackson's lips twisted. "Boston and Abigail O'Conner ruined all of it for me. I'm ready for a different life."

Chet leaned back and folded his arms. "You're a good doctor, and you've got talent. The boy would have died if not for you."

"Maybe he should have," Jackson muttered. "It would have saved me a load of grief. I wouldn't have gotten arrested, and I would still have Caroline."

"Are you sure she's who you want? Seems to me your Caroline had no sand. If she can let a little thing like that discourage her, she isn't worth having."

Jackson met his dad's steady gaze. "Aiding and abetting a criminal isn't a little thing. It's a felony. My name went all over Boston. All my patients transferred to other doctors. My practice died. No one wanted to associate with me. I couldn't go anywhere without someone recognizing me."

Chet shrugged this time. "If it weren't Richard O'Conner, it would have been something else. Your Caroline didn't love you. If she did, she would have stuck by your side through it all."

Jackson closed weary eyes. "She said she didn't know me anymore. I wasn't the man she fell in love with."

"That's what I am saying, son. She didn't love you."

Deep down, he knew it all along. Caroline accepted Jackson's proposal because it suited her daddy to have a brilliant surgeon as a son-in-law. It was time to move on.

"So can I stay for a while?" Jackson picked up his fork and tucked into the bacon and eggs on his plate.

Chet chuckled. "Long as you don't eat all my food, sure." There was plenty, and they both knew it. "The fact is, we could use another investor in the livery. We need to repaint and repair some of the stalls."

"Invest in the livery?"

Chet nodded. "That's right. I offered a partnership to Buck Standish two years ago. He's been so busy helping his wife at the bakery, I never see him. I could use your help, and the livery could use your money. I'm offering you half of my piece."

Jackson jumped at the chance. He invested all the money he saved from his practice. Buck agreed to the terms and offered Jackson half of his piece as well. Jackson shook hands with them both and became the leading shareholder of the livery stable. He owned half. Buck Standish and his dad owned the other half.

All of this happened more than a year ago. Jackson was glad he came to Wylder when he did. He wished he would have come sooner. Chet Daniels died of a heart attack four months after Jackson settled in.

Jackson sighed. Today marked the anniversary of his dad's death. He missed Chet every day.

"How are you holding up?"

Jackson stopped and leaned on his pitchfork. Buck Standish walked toward him, carrying a tow-headed little boy. Tall and lean with dark hair, Buck and his wife, Cissy, had a one-year-old son. The boy went everywhere with him.

"Good as can be expected," Jackson replied.

Buck Standish was a famous gunfighter turned citizen. He was an honest, hard-working man, and

Jackson trusted him.

"I came to see if you wanted to visit your dad's grave. I could watch the livery for a spell."

Jackson shook his head. "That's mighty kind of you, but Dad and I said all we had to say in the months before his death. Makes it easier to bear."

Buck nodded his head. "You're one of the lucky ones. My dad and I were never friends."

Jackson nodded and began to pitch hay once more.

Buck watched him for a minute or two. "You hear about the gent who got shot in the back halfway to Lonetree?"

"I did," Jackson answered. "They figure out who did it?"

Buck shook his head. "I talked to a stranger today at the bakery who said the dead man's family hired him to investigate the murder. He came in on the train. He wants to search Wylder for the killer."

Jackson stilled. "You saying the killer came here?"

Buck shrugged. "We aren't far from where the man was murdered. Have you seen any strangers around?"

Jackson shook his head. "Nothing unusual." Except he had seen something unusual. He had a wounded woman in his back room who had been shot the same night and in the back.

Buck nodded as he shifted the boy to his other arm. "Let me know if you need any help."

"Will do." Jackson waited until Buck disappeared around the open livery doors. Then he went to check on Miss Jones.

Chapter Four

William Smythe stood outside the Five Star Saloon
and looked up and down the street. Things were quiet in
Wylder. Farmers and cowhands milled about. He rolled
a cigarette and lit it. Whoever shot Rex Conway was a
clever son of a bitch. He came across Rex's body on his
way out to the cabin. If William came ten minutes
earlier, he would have caught the bastard in the act. He
got the son of a bitch as he rode away. William fired his
pistol and struck gold. He found blood along the trail in
several places.

He had a hell of a time following the trail. Once the
murderer ran into the dry creek bed, he crossed and re-
crossed his path, making it a pain in the ass to follow.
He didn't understand how the murdering bastard knew
the countryside. He had to be the luckiest man alive, or
he knew Lonetree like the back of his hand. A local
man, William thought. But who?

William lost him in the dark. When he came back
at first light, he couldn't make sense of the prints he
found. He followed a trail east to Cheyenne. He wasted
valuable time hunting down all the doctors and making
them talk. There were a lot of bullet wounds, but none
of their patients were shot in the back.

A smile twisted William's lip. Rex offered to bring
one of the new whores out to the cabin, but when they
questioned Miss Gwen's girls, one of them were

talking. The whore named Sadie disappeared into thin air. All the persuasion he and his friends could muster didn't make the others talk. Miss Gwen took exception to their methods and had the sheriff escort him and his friends out of town. The sheriff pocketed the money Bernard Smythe gave him for not arresting William and told William and his friends not to come back. William rode five miles out of town and sent Porter and James to Cheyenne to see if they could find Sadie. She couldn't have gone too far. She had little or no money. Miss Gwen kept most of what her girls earned. So far, Porter and James hadn't had any luck finding the girl.

William struck a match and cupped his hand around the flame until his cigarette lit. He inhaled and blew out a puff of smoke. Wylder was the next closest town. He'd turn the place upside-down if he had to. There were three places a stranger visited when he came to town, the local saloon, the hotel, and the livery. William smiled. They were all on his list. A bullet wound required a doctor. Doc Sullivan had an office on the north end of town. William dragged on his cigarette. He had a room at the Wylder Hotel, located on the north end of town too. He planned to visit Doc Sullivan and find out about any bullet wounds he treated in the last week or so. Since Wylder Hotel was a couple of doors down from the doc's place. He would notice the patients who came and went. William stepped on his cigarette and strolled down Sidewinder Lane toward the hotel. The doc's office and the little bakery appeared at the end of the road. Rex had been a friend. He would find the man who shot him and cut him into little pieces.

****

Maryanne woke with a start. What time was it? More important, what day was it? She looked over at the little window on the north wall. Dust particles floated in the air. The waning sunlight told her it was late afternoon. Maryanne frowned. A train rumbled down the tracks. It blew a whistle signaling its arrival at the station. A bell rang, and the steam engine hissed. She'd wasted a lot of time sleeping when she should have been leaving. The longer she hung around Wylder, the more her chance of being discovered. She had to high-tail it out of here.

She sat up and scooted to the edge of the single bed. She hurt like blue blazes. Maryanne bit her lip and waited for the pain to ease. She put her hands down on either side to hold herself steady. The room spun around and around. Her head pounded with pain. Nausea rose in her throat.

Someone tapped on her door, and then Mr. Daniels strolled inside. He brought the scent of hay, leather, and soup. Maryanne looked up.

"Miss Jones, you'll tear your wounds open," he scolded. He placed a tray on the table beside the bed and walked toward her. He lifted the bedclothes and swung her legs back under them. "Why are you so determined to get up? If you don't give yourself time to heal, you'll regret it. The more you move around, the longer you're going to take to get well. You weren't awake at lunch, and I thought you might be hungry. So, I brought some soup."

"How long have I been here?" Maryanne asked. Her throat was so dry it hurt to talk.

"A little more than a week. You lost a lot of blood."

"I'm thirsty," Maryanne croaked.

He picked up a metal pitcher and poured her a glass of water.

She scooted back, angling herself into a half-sitting position. Lord, she ached. She took the glass from him, but her hand trembled so hard the water spilled over the side.

"Here," Mr. Daniels said. He sat on the edge of her bed and let her lean against him while he helped her drink.

Maryanne shook so hard she could barely swallow. Oh, but the water felt good. The cool liquid soothed her throat. She drank and drank. Once finished, she leaned back. The heat of his body and the broad expanse of his chest enveloped her. He was warm, solid, and muscular. Maryanne froze. Fear settled in her stomach. She cringed out of habit and waited. Nothing happened. His body warmed her, his scent calmed her, and her fear drifted away. She could feel every breath he drew. Maryanne leaned forward to put some space between them.

Mr. Daniels rose to his feet and faced her. His gaze met hers. They stared at each other.

She could look at him all day and not get tired of it. His hazel eyes changed color with the light. They sucked her in until she drowned in their depths. Awareness hummed through her. He was so different from William. She was safe with him so close. Something she never felt with William. Time stood still.

A horse snorted out in the livery, and Maryanne jumped. Mr. Daniels's gaze roamed over her face and settled on her lips.

Maryanne looked down. She had never been drawn to a man as she was to Mr. Daniels, and she was conscious of every move he made. She shivered and licked her lips. "I don't know why my hand is shaking so bad."

"I do. You've been shot. It'll take time to feel like yourself again." He pulled a gold watch from his pocket and picked up her wrist.

Maryanne swallowed. His fingers were warm and firm. Trembling, she stared at his face while he looked at his watch. Mr. Daniels was a good man, honest and kind. She closed her eyes and breathed in deep. Mr. Daniels smelled like coffee, sunshine, and security. For the first time in her life, she didn't hate being female.

"Your heart is beating a little fast. You need to drink more water. You could be dehydrated from blood loss."

Maryanne put a hand to her head. "My head feels like it's going to crack open."

Mr. Daniels nodded. "I imagine so. It goes along with the dehydration. I can ask Doc Sullivan for some morphine."

"No," Maryanne responded. "I don't want anyone to know I'm here."

"I know," Mr. Daniels said. "There must have been a full moon the night you got shot. Today I learned the bank in Lonetree got robbed. We haven't had this much crime in a while."

There *had been* a full moon. She used it to guide her mare to Wylder. "Do they know who did it?" she whispered. The water helped some, and she wanted more. She waited to see what Mr. Daniels had to say. Her heart pounded in time with her head.

"No." Mr. Daniels shook his head. "There are a lot of people out looking for Rex Conway's killer. Wylder is full of strangers."

"Why?" she managed to ask.

"The reward money. Word got out, and every bounty hunter in the area rode in to see if they can get lucky."

Maryanne choked. She bent forward to get some air.

Mr. Daniels stood beside her. He leaned in close to look at her face. "Are you all right, Miss Jones?"

She nodded. Her hands shook. She couldn't look him in the eye.

"You need to rest," he said. "There is soup if you're hungry." He turned to go. "I'll be back in a while to check on you."

Maryanne slid back beneath the covers and closed her eyes. Tension stretched across her forehead. She didn't have the strength to deal with this. She wanted to get dressed and get the hell out of Wylder before someone figured it out. For a thousand dollars, her own grandmother would be tempted to turn her in. If they thought the murderer was a man, she had a little time. Her eyelids drooped. Lord, she was so tired. Maybe she should rest, but just for a minute.

****

Jackson smiled when he peeked inside her room a while later. Miss Jones lie on her side with her left hand under her cheek, asleep. She needed her rest. He wondered about her reaction every time he talked about the murder. She knew more than she said. He would bet his last empty stall on it. He gazed at her face. She was such a tiny thing. His granny would say she needed meat and potatoes. He thought about the way she felt when he helped her drink. Her soft woman's curves felt right in his arms. She smelled of lavender. Jackson wondered what she would do if he kissed her. He wanted to. For a minute or two, when he held her, he thought about turning her around and holding her close.

He wondered what she tasted like. Her sweet pink lips tempted him to find out. His mind returned to the morning he found her. He never knew a woman who dressed in man's breeches. They accentuated the curve of her backside, drawing his attention there while he helped her out of her clothes. Miss Jones possessed a perfect woman's body. He wanted to cup her backside against him while he plundered her soft lips.

Miss Jones murmured in her sleep, bringing him back to the present.

Jackson frowned and walked from the room. He shook his head, disgusted with his thoughts. Miss Jones needed protection from whoever shot her. She also needed to heal. He shouldn't have improper thoughts about her, but he did. He would do well to remember she was engaged. Jackson grimaced. He could not get involved with her. He wasn't the kind of man to take what didn't belong to him.

Jackson sent Tom out to check on the horses in the yard. He grabbed the pitchfork from its place on the wall and went to throw some hay. Physical exercise would get his mind off Miss Jones. He worked up a sweat in no time. Jackson rolled his shoulders and grinned as he fed and watered the horses.

"You Jackson Daniels?" the man's voice came from outside the stall.

Jackson looked up. "I am. What can I do for you?"

A thin man with dark hair and a tall hat stood beside the stall gate. He had on a black, broadcloth jacket, a silk shirt, and machine-woven pants. A black necktie formed a bow at his throat. His expensive leather boots shone in the light coming in the windows overhead. "My name is William Smythe. I have a couple of questions to ask you." He took a cigarette from his pocket and lit it.

Jackson leaned on his pitchfork and held his hand out. You could tell a lot about a man by the way he clasped your hand. Mr. Smythe's handshake resembled a dead fish. He had no muscle. His hands were soft like a woman's. Jackson looked the man over from head to toe. Mr. Smythe's attire screamed a city slicker with money to burn. "Go ahead. What do you want to know?" He took Mr. Smythe's measure. The twist of his lips conveyed cruelty. His shifty eyes told Jackson not to trust him.

Mr. Smythe blew a perfect circle of smoke. "I am looking for someone." He stared at Jackson.

Jackson stared back and waited. He wouldn't trust Mr. Smythe with a wheel barrel of horse manure.

"A friend of mine was killed a week ago, shot in the back between here and Lonetree. Wylder is riding distance from the site of the murder. I figure you run the livery. You saw something. I want to know what you've seen."

Jackson didn't move. "I see lots of strangers. They come, drop their horses off, and leave. You got a description for the man you're looking for?"

"I shot him as he rode away."

Jackson stiffened. *In the back?* "Anything else?"

Mr. Smythe drew on his cigarette. "No. I didn't see

his face, just his silhouette."

Suspicion filled Jackson. Was this one of the bastards looking for Miss Jones? "Sorry, friend. I haven't seen a man with a bullet wound." He spoke the truth. Miss Jones was a woman. "You should check with Doc Sullivan. His office is on the north end of town. He'd know if anyone has been shot."

Mr. Smythe blew another circle of smoke. "Perhaps you don't know who I am." Mr. Smythe's smile didn't reach his eyes. "My father owns Smythe Bank and Trust out of New York City." He paused as if to let the words sink in. "I want the man who murdered my friend. I will find him, and when I do, he will pay for his crime. I'm a man with a long memory. If you help me locate the killer, you will be rewarded. If I find out you've lied to me…Let's just say you'll wish you never laid eyes on me."

Jackson smiled and leaned against the stall railing. "Are you threatening me?" he asked. His voice dropped silky soft. A good old-fashioned fist fight would sure make him feel better. He wanted to erase the smile from Mr. Smythe's face. He knew about city boys and their money.

Mr. Smythe raised an eyebrow. "I wouldn't dream of it. I do, however, suggest you give me the information I want." He ran his gloved hand down the rail in front of him. He glanced at Jackson. "How much money do you think it would take to replace all these horses?"

Jackson shrugged. "I don't worry about it too much. A lot of people would be mighty upset if anything happened to this livery. It wouldn't take them long to figure out who did it. People in Wylder don't take to strangers." He rolled his shoulders to loosen his muscles. He hoped the banker's son wanted to get right to it. He hadn't had a good fight in ages.

Mr. Smythe smiled again and stepped back. "I'm curious, nothing more. No harm meant." He clasped his hands in front of him. "I'll be at the Wylder Hotel if you decide you want to talk."

Jackson returned stare for stare until Mr. Smythe dropped his gaze. He was through with the city slicker and his posturing. Jackson turned his back on Mr. Smythe and picked up his pitchfork. The man was a bully. Jackson hoped he took exception to his dismissal. He wanted to beat the man to a pulp. No one threatened him or his livery.

A moment of silence followed. "If I find out you're lying to me, you'll be sorry."

Jackson didn't look up. "You can see yourself out."

He listened to the dandy walk away. Jackson seethed. He ran into men of Mr. Smythe's caliber in Boston. Miss Jones had every right to be worried. There were a lot of unsavory characters about. If the men who shot her were as bad as Mr. Smythe, she should stay out of sight. He frowned. He wasn't convinced Mr. Smythe wasn't one of them. Jackson knew Miss Jones hadn't told him the truth about her wound. She knew more than she said. He should have taken her to Doc Sullivan, but after meeting Mr. Smythe, he was glad he didn't. Whoever shot her would have no problem finding her if he had.

"Do you think he'll make trouble for us?" Tom stood next to the stall. He stared after Mr. Smythe.

"If he does, he picked the wrong man to start a fight with." Jackson turned to Tom. "I want to know if he comes snooping around again."

Tom nodded and grabbed a pitchfork. They worked side by side until the horses were all fed and watered. When they were done, Tom walked toward the door. "See you tomorrow, Jackson."

"Watch yourself. If you have any trouble with Mr. Smythe, you let me know," Jackson called after him.

"Will do," Tom said, and walked away.

Jackson put the tools away and washed his face and hands. He left a pot of stock on the stove in his rooms. He cut potatoes and carrots into the base and added a few dried herbs. He thickened the soup with flour. When it was done, he ladled some into a bowl for Miss Jones. He filled a bowl for himself and set them both on a tray. He left his rooms and walked along the stalls until he reached Miss Jones' door. He peeked inside. She sat up in her bed with the fire poker in her hands. Her eyes were wide and frightened in her pale face.

Jackson looked around. "What's going on?" He set the tray by the bed.

Miss Jones shook her head and let the poker slide to the floor. She lay down with a groan. " I heard voices."

"There's nothing to worry about. A stranger came in asking questions. He's gone now. No one knows you're here."

"Who is he? What did he want?" Maryanne licked her lips.

She must be thirsty again. He poured her another glass of water.

She lifted herself up to take the glass. Jackson slid behind her and helped her until she pushed it away. Strangers must frighten her. Miss Jones trembled like an autumn leaf in the breeze.

He laid her back against the pillow. "Mr. Smythe asked about a gunshot cowboy. I sent him to Doc Sullivan."

Miss Jones stiffened and paled a bit more. "Mr. Smythe?"

"I won't let anyone hurt you," he said. "Do you want to tell me what happened?"

Miss Jones lifted tortured eyes to his. "I did. My father wants me to marry a horrible man. I…ran away…and got involved in something I shouldn't. I got shot in the process." Her big blue eyes looked up at him. She swallowed a sob. "I can't go back. Please don't make me."

"I might run a livery, but I am a gentleman." One wouldn't know it by the thoughts going through his head every time he looked at her. Jackson kept his gaze on her face. He didn't want her to notice he knew the front of her nightgown came unbuttoned while she slept. He didn't want her to know how sexy he thought she was with her hair messed up and a blush on her cheeks. Jackson stared at her mouth. He shouldn't think about kissing her soft lips, either. He cleared his throat. "I brought you some dinner."

Miss Jones gazed up at him. "Thank you, Mr. Daniels."

Jackson propped some pillows behind her and handed her a bowl of soup. "There isn't anything to be embarrassed about, Miss Jones. We all make mistakes." He took his own bowl of soup and told her about Miss Abigail O'Conner.

Chapter Five

"I had a busy practice in Boston as an up-and-coming surgeon. Everyone wanted my opinion. I consulted with brilliant surgeons on a regular basis. I had my life mapped out, or so I thought. I planned to marry Caroline Miller, daughter of Boston's mayor, Bradley Miller." Mr. Daniels took a bite of soup.

Maryanne studied his face. He loved Miss Miller. She could tell by the way his voice softened when he said her name.

"A young woman stopped me in the street one day. She said her name was Abigail O'Conner. She claimed her brother had been shot protecting her honor. She pleaded with me to help. I had a dinner party to attend at the mayor's house, with Caroline. Miss Abigail begged. I told her to take him to the hospital. She said they had no money, and her brother would die if I didn't come." Mr. Daniels sighed. "I sent a message to Caroline telling her I would be late. Then I went to help Miss O'Conner's brother. She took me to a cheap hotel. Her brother lay on the bed soaked in blood. The bullet went in deep. It took me three hours to dig it out. When I finished, I bandaged him and told Miss O'Conner to keep a close eye on him. I promised to return the next day."

Mr. Daniels spooned more soup into his mouth. "Caroline was furious with me. Her father had important people for me to meet, and I never arrived. I went to apologize to the mayor and discovered a priceless painting from the Museum of Fine Arts had been stolen. The chief of police was in the mayor's office giving details of the robbery. His men were out looking for it. The villain had been shot during the pursuit.

"I told Mayor Miller I would come by later to talk. I promised Caroline I would make it up to her and went to check on Richard O'Conner. I surprised them. Miss O'Conner had a carpet bag on the bed filled with their clothes. Mr. O'Conner was pale but doing well. Miss O'Conner and her brother were fidgety. I could not figure out why, until I caught sight of a square object. The stolen painting from the museum sat beside the door. I turned to leave and never made it. The police burst into the hotel room and arrested me along with the O'Conner's."

Mr. Daniels rubbed his face. "They charged me with aiding and abetting a criminal. No one believed my protests of innocence because the painting was in plain sight. Caroline broke off the engagement. I lost my practice and my good name. No one wanted me to consult anymore. My reputation lay in ruins. All my patients were transferred to other doctors."

Maryanne stared at him. "So what did you do?"

Mr. Daniels smiled. "I spent a month in jail before my lawyer convinced the judge I had nothing to do with it. When I got out, I came to Wylder."

Maryanne digested his story. "But you didn't do anything wrong."

Mr. Daniels nodded. "They caught me in the wrong place at the right time." He gazed at her. "Sometimes bad things happen." He studied her face. "I understand if the same sort of thing happened to you."

Maryanne trembled. Would he believe her if she told him the truth?

"Did you see who shot Mr. Conway?" He searched her face for several seconds.

Maryanne shook her head.

"Mr. Smythe said Mr. Conway was his friend. He wants the man responsible," Jackson murmured. "I wonder if you came across the murder and didn't know it."

Maryanne froze. She hadn't recovered from the first time Mr. Daniels mentioned William. Mr. Daniels came too close to the truth for comfort. "To do that, I would have to be in the vicinity," Maryanne said. "I focused on running away and didn't see anybody else." She cringed at the lie. If he found out the truth, he would kick her out of his spare room, and she would never see him again. Maryanne bit her lip and gazed down at her trembling hands.

"Someone is out there shooting people. Mr. Conway got shot from behind, and so did you. Real men don't shoot people in the back." Mr. Daniels shook his head. "There are two things I do not tolerate— cowards and thieves. In my mind, they are the same. The only thing worse than a murderer is a horse thief. Think how much better off we'd be if they were all in prison or strung up."

Maryanne's heart plummeted. She sipped her soup. She was both. For one minute there, she thought he might understand.

"I wonder if the fellow who robbed the bank came upon Rex Conway and shot him, then ran across you."

He mused for several minutes.

Maryanne's heart did double-time. She swallowed, hoping her heart would drop back into her chest.

Mr. Daniels glanced at her face. His voice softened. "I won't let them hurt you, Miss Jones."

She nodded to let him know she understood. She set her soup back on the tray and slid down into the bed. "Thank you for the food and for letting me stay here, Mr. Daniels."

He cleared his throat. "Call me Jackson. My friends do."

Maryanne looked up. "Are we friends?"

"I'd say we are. I don't dig bullets out of just anybody." He grinned. "Not anymore."

Maryanne gazed at him. She would be his friend. She would be anything he wanted if he kept looking at her the way he did. "You can call me Maryanne."

Jackson set his empty bowl on the tray. "Try to get some rest, Maryanne. I'll be close by if you need anything." He rose to his feet and strolled toward the door with the tray in his hands. "You're safe here."

She knew it without being told. "Goodnight, Jackson." She smiled when she said his name. She drifted off, thinking about the way he said her name. Jackson made her feel special. William made her feel dirty.

They talked often over the next couple of weeks as Maryanne recuperated. Her strength came back, and the color returned to her cheeks. They shared a lot of the same thoughts and tastes. Maryanne discovered they also shared the same sense of humor. William didn't return. Maryanne thanked God every night in her prayers, but she knew it wasn't over. With him in town, she had to plan her exit and soon. Otherwise, the robbery and her escape would all be for naught.

The third week she stayed at the livery, Jackson invited her to the little kitchen in his rooms while he prepared dinner. Maryanne never ventured to the kitchen at home. Papa had a cook. So watching Jackson cook was a novelty. He made a meal of fried salt pork and potatoes. He cooked up some fresh peas one of his customers gave him and made a pot of coffee. Maryanne told him about life at home. She didn't mention her father's name or where she lived. She kept details to a minimum. Jackson smiled at her anecdotes and urged her on when she stopped without finishing her story.

Maryanne enjoyed being around Jackson more than she wanted to admit. She looked forward to his step outside her door. She loved the way he made her feel small when he stood beside her bed. She loved the scent of hay, sunshine, and leather on his clothes. Jackson would bring her dinner and tell her of the day he had. She would listen and eat, content to be close to him. When he smiled at her, Maryanne melted. Being female wasn't a bad thing around Jackson.

In the middle of the next week, Maryanne decided to get up. She felt better, and an idea took root. All day she listened to customers coming and going. The livery was at capacity. Jackson would be tired and hungry by the time the livery closed for the day. She could make some soup and surprise him. She had to leave, and soon. But Maryanne couldn't go without doing something to show Jackson how much she appreciated him and his kindness. Whenever she planned the date to leave Wylder, she got a stone in her chest. She cherished the time she spent with Jackson. She hated the thought of leaving.

Maryanne stood beside her valise and looked from her borrowed breeches and shirt to her dresses hanging on hooks. For the first time, she wanted to look pretty. She touched the sleeve of her new pink gingham dress. Would Jackson like her in this?

Papa never noticed what she wore, and William was the last person on earth she wanted to attract. When William noticed her, pain followed.

Maryanne ran her hand over the fabric of her dress. She had the new dress for almost two months and had not bothered to put it on. She hadn't wanted to until now. Maryanne lifted the pink gingham dress from the hook and retrieved fresh underwear from her valise. She bit her lip with indecision. Then again, with William in town, it might be better to dress in the cowboy's breeches. If he recognized her, it would be catastrophic.

Jackson didn't know William was the man her father wanted her to marry, and Maryanne wanted to keep it that way. She picked the shirt up and sniffed. It smelled like lye soap and sunshine. So did the borrowed breeches. Jackson didn't deserve to be dragged into the middle of the mess she made. The soup would be her way of telling him how much she appreciated him helping her.

Maryanne thought of his wavy dark hair and hazel eyes. She shoved the shirt and breeches back into the valise and set the pink gingham dress on her bed. She wanted Jackson to see her dressed as a girl before he learned about the terrible things she had done.

She got as far as her corset but could not lace it up.

The pressure of her undergarment reminded her the wound wasn't healed yet. Sighing, Maryanne hung the dress back on the peg and pulled on the stolen breeches and shirt. She plaited her hair and pinned it down. Then she dusted the cowboy hat off and set it in her head. It was for the best. If someone saw her, they wouldn't look twice.

She peeked around the door at the empty livery and smiled with relief. Maryanne walked down the wooden floor toward Jackson's rooms. She came across a man with a pitchfork cleaning out the stalls. He had black hair and green eyes, of medium height and good looking in a rugged way.

"Can I help you?" he asked.

"I'm looking for Jackson Daniels." She lowered her voice and sauntered around the corner in what she hoped passed for a man's swagger.

"He went out on a call. A farmer cannot get his cow to deliver, so he sent for Jackson. Want me to give him a message?"

Maryanne shook her head. "No." She walked close to one of the stalls and looked at the mare laying in the straw. "Are any of these horses for sale?" She toyed with the idea of purchasing one. She planned to buy a train ticket for California as soon as possible. If she bought a horse beforehand, it would throw them off her trail once they figured it all out. She could pay for the mare to ride in the livestock car, and she would have a way to travel once she arrived at her destination.

The man leaned on his pitchfork. "We got a bay mare who needs a new home. Some cowboy left her here nigh on three weeks ago. We boarded her and didn't get paid. Jackson would be the one to ask."

"Mind if I take a look?" a voice said from the livery door.

Maryanne froze. *William came back!* Her stomach lurched. It was too late to run. She tugged her hat forward and kept her chin down.

"She's right there." The livery man pointed to the stall next to Maryanne.

William strolled toward her, and Maryanne quit breathing. She plucked a piece of straw and chewed on the end like the men who sat around the mercantile in Lonetree. She hoped she looked natural. Maryanne tucked her hands into the pockets of her breeches and adopted a man's stance. She had soft girl hands. Jackson told her he noticed them the morning he found her. William might too.

William let himself into the stall. "A friend of mine got shot between here and Lonetree. I'm looking for the bastard who murdered him. What did the cowboy look like who owned this horse? Was he wounded?" William studied the mare's hooves.

Maryanne sat as still as stone. Her skin crawled when William's gaze dropped to her. What in God's name would she do if he recognized her? Perspiration dampened her brow.

Jackson's man shrugged. "I wasn't here when the mare came in ." He pushed his hat back and stared at William. "I don't recall Jackson saying anything about a wounded man. You'll have to ask him the particulars."

"I did," William said. "I hoped you would be more forthcoming." He let himself out of the stall and glanced around the livery as if checking for witnesses. His hand dropped toward the pistol on his side.

Maryanne gulped. She knew William had no respect for the law. Never once had he paid for any crime he committed. His daddy and their lawyers helped him walk away every time. But would he kill a man in cold blood? She swallowed hard and pulled the straw from her mouth with shaking hands.

"The man I am looking for was shot in the back," William said. He walked toward the livery worker. His hand fondled the butt of his gun.

Jackson's man didn't blink. He held his ground. "I told you, I wasn't here. If I were you, I'd ask Doc Sullivan."

William stared at the man for long minutes. "The doc wouldn't talk either. He claimed he hadn't seen a gunshot wound in more than a month." William pulled the gun from its holster.

Maryanne's heart stopped beating. She glanced back the way she came. She gauged the distance to her room. If William started shooting, she wanted an exit strategy.

"Someone in Wylder knows something. The man I'm looking for lost a lot of blood. I trailed him enough to know. He didn't go east, or I would've found him. Wylder is the first town to the west." He waved the gun around. "Tell Jackson Daniels I'll be back. I'm not done with him yet." He pointed his gun at the hired hand and spun the chamber.

Jackson's man didn't move.

William laughed and holstered his gun.

How did William know she got shot unless he shot her? The room tilted.

William glanced at Maryanne on his way out. "You have to eat more than straw, kid, if you want to grow to be a man."

Maryanne choked. She didn't. She wanted to grow to be a wealthy, single female on her way to the Orient. She wouldn't go anywhere if William figured out who she was.

Maryanne waited five more minutes to be sure William left for good. "I will find Jackson later," she mumbled and wandered around the stalls until the man's attention was elsewhere. She made sure she was alone at the back of the livery before she slipped through her door. She didn't want to take any chances with William snooping around. Maryanne forgot about the soup.

Sometime later, a sharp knock sounded on her door. Maryanne grabbed the poker from the fire and peeked out.

Jackson stood there with a tray of food. "Can I come in?"

Maryanne stepped back to allow him to enter.

Jackson set the tray on the little table. "I heard we had a visitor." He frowned. "And Tom tells me a young man came in asking for me. Did you go out into the livery today?"

At her nod, he continued, "If you don't want the townsfolk to know you're here, you need to stay out of sight." He leaned against the little table and folded his arms.

Maryanne nodded her head. "I needed a little fresh air, so I stepped out for a minute."

"You shouldn't be so reckless. You knew there were strangers around."

She dropped her chin. "I didn't think he would be back," she murmured. "I thought I would make you some supper and got distracted by the horses."

Jackson handed her a plate containing a sandwich and an apple. "You need to focus on getting well. I can handle the food." His gaze searched her face. "Mr. Smythe has been all over town asking questions. There is a new fellow here, too. He's short, middle-aged, wears a flat hat and glasses. He says he's a detective and works for the Conway family."

Maryanne's heart skipped a beat. "I'll stay out of sight." She picked up the sandwich with a shaky hand.

Jackson walked toward her. He tilted her face up so he could gaze into her eyes. "I won't let anyone hurt you." His warm breath blew across her cheeks.

Maryanne swallowed. His nearness sent butterflies skittering through her. She shivered in response.

"But you have to do your part and stay inside when I'm not here."

The heat of his body called to her like a moth to the lantern. She sniffed. He smelled wonderful, like sunshine and freedom. Maryanne swayed toward him. She looked at his lips so close to hers and wondered what he kissed like. William frightened her. His lips were brutal, hard, and cold. His kisses hurt, and she didn't like being forced. Sometimes he left bruises on her jaw where he held her while he ground his lips into hers.

She bet Jackson's would be different. She looked up at him.

His eyes darkened as he gazed at her. He stared at her mouth as he leaned forward.

Maryanne closed her eyes in anticipation. She lifted her face, eager for his kiss.

A sharp knock caused her to jump. She opened her

eyes in alarm. Jackson stepped away from her with what looked like regret in his eyes. He slipped out the door and closed it behind him.

"Jackson, the sheriff wants to have a word with you," Tom's voice said from the other side of the door.

Maryanne listened to their boots thump on the wooden floor as they walked away. Perspiration broke out on her brow. She should have left the second her wound quit bleeding. Fear wound around like a snake inside her belly. She tempted fate by hanging around Wylder. Too bad she didn't tempt Jackson as well. Maryanne bit her lip. Being a girl had possibilities, but she needed to leave. She hadn't worked out the details on how she planned to buy a train ticket without being seen. Maryanne glanced at the bed with her saddlebags hidden beneath. She had to lug them along with her. Why did escaping have to be so hard? She should be sailing across the ocean by now, headed to new horizons. Instead, she wasted valuable time because she got shot. Then there was Jackson. She wished everything were different so she could find out if he liked her as much as she liked him.

Chapter Six

Maryanne rose the next morning and dressed in her pink gingham. If her day of reckoning had come, she wanted to look her best. She put her corset on and laced it up. After ten minutes of agony, she took it off again. She used her binding to disguise the fact. Women who walked around without all their underwear were whores. At least, that's what Papa said. Maryanne decided she didn't care. She brushed her hair out and plaited it. At home, she would have pulled the sides up and curled the back. It wasn't possible here.

A sharp knock at the door caused her to jump. She laid her brush down and turned toward the sound.

"Are you awake?" Jackson's voice came through the door.

This is it. With a lump in her throat, she opened the door. She expected to see the sheriff. Instead, Jackson stood there with a tray of breakfast.

"Can I come in?" His gaze traveled over her.

Maryanne nodded and stepped aside.

Jackson strode into the room and set the tray on the table. "How are you feeling today?"

Maryanne took a deep breath. "I feel wonderful. In fact, I feel so wonderful I would like to buy one of your horses and be on my way," she gushed. Relief flooded through her when she realized Jackson came alone. She said what she wanted to say, and the seed had been planted.

Jackson observed her for several seconds. "You look good." His gaze roamed over her hair, her lips, her breasts, her hips, and back to her face. "Beautiful," he murmured. "But not well enough to travel." He searched her face. Disappointment shone from his eyes. "Where are you headed? I don't think you ever said."

She clutched her hands together in front of her. "I have family in California," she lied. "I planned to go there until Papa came to his senses."

Jackson frowned. "So you plan to ride all the way to California? Alone?" His eyebrows rose.

"Well, yes," Maryanne admitted. When he put it like that, it sounded foolish. "That's why I want to buy a horse."

"I don't need to tell you the dangers of a woman traveling alone." He indicated the bullet wound in her side. "Worse can happen, you know. The next man you meet might not care if you're someone else's girl." He searched her face. "Tell you what, why don't you stick around until you feel better, and then I'll buy you a train ticket to California."

Maryanne blinked. "I can take care of myself." A train ride to California happened to be on her list of things to do. She hesitated. Maybe she should let him buy it and switch at the last minute. What's the worst that could happen?

Jackson shook his head. "I don't think so. There are bad men out there, Maryanne. You're a beautiful woman. Any number of things could happen." He looked her over. Jackson ran a hand through his hair and gazed at her for several seconds. "If I were honest with you, I would tell you I want you to stay in

Wylder."

Maryanne's heart rate increased. "Why?"

He stared at her. "Because I like you."

Maryanne wanted to do a jig. "I like you, too." She smiled at him and took a step toward him.

Jackson shook his head in response. "You belong to someone else, Maryanne, and I don't poach."

Maryanne gaped in surprise. "Papa made the arrangement, not me. I didn't agree to it. I never said 'I do' or 'yes' or anything else. I don't belong to anybody because nobody asked me."

Jackson shook his head. "It doesn't matter. Your father gave his word."

Maryanne's spirits plummeted. "I should have known you'd think like them. Is that why you don't kiss me?"

Jackson looked surprised. "I don't kiss you because I am a gentleman. And yes because you are engaged to another man."

Maryanne gave a cry of outrage. "I am a grown woman, and I can make my own decisions. Nobody owns me. I own myself." She marched over to him while he digested her comments and threw her arms around his neck. She planted her lips on his and kissed the hell out of him.

Jackson stiffened, but he didn't push her away. Encouraged, she softened against him, reveling in the feel of his lips against hers. She slid her lips back and forth across his. His lips were firm and tasted like heaven. Maryanne sighed with delight. She knew kissing him would be different than kissing William. She pulled him closer.

Jackson's arms clamped around her waist. His

hands slid up her back until he cradled her head in his hand. His mouth opened over hers, and he kissed her back. Maryanne melted against him. Her knees turned to jelly. When Jackson slid his tongue into her mouth, she grabbed his shoulders to keep herself upright. He deepened the kiss and drank from her lips until both were breathing heavy.

He lifted his head and gazed into her eyes. "I like you, Maryanne. Everything about you tantalizes me, but I'm not a thief. I can't take what belongs to someone else." He caressed the side of her face. "I promised to keep you safe, and I will. To do so, no one can know you're here. I'll continue bringing you food and checking on you, but the kissing can't happen again." He looked regretful when he said the words. "You have to promise me you won't get too close. If I lost my self-control with you, I'd never forgive myself." Jackson set her from him and walked toward the door.

Maryanne trembled. He liked her! She smiled, and hope blossomed inside her. He kissed her back. Her stomach quivered in response. If only things were different.

Harsh reality stomped across her mind. She couldn't stay. Not with all the things she did. One thought led to another. "What did the sheriff want? Did it have something to do with Mr. Smythe?"

Jackson stopped with his hand on the latch. "The man who robbed the bank in Lonetree stole a horse from the saloon to make his getaway. Sheriff Wylder asked the same questions everybody else asked."

"And?" Maryanne whispered. She lifted her gaze to his. She equated dread with William. It had no place in her life when it came to Jackson. Yet here it came, rearing its ugly head inside her.

Jackson sighed. "I told Sheriff Wylder I didn't see anything suspicious."

Maryanne blew out a breath of relief. "Thank you."

"We don't know who shot you or why. We know whoever it is has no honor, not if he shoots people in the back. We also don't know if your fiancé is out looking for you. Common sense suggests he is. Both of which are excellent reasons for you to stay out of sight." His gaze caught hers. "I'll be by later." He shut the door.

Maryanne sank onto the bed and buried her face in her arms. She put Jackson in jeopardy by staying here. Originally, she planned to buy a train ticket for California and breeze through Wylder. Because of her, Jackson harbored a criminal. He lied to protect her. She was a thief and a murderer. Would Sheriff Wylder charge Jackson with aiding and abetting a criminal like the law in Boston? Maryanne curled up in a little ball. She meant to escape William and a life of torture. She never wanted to involve Jackson or anybody else. Jackson would never forgive her for lying to him. She would never forgive herself if he were arrested because of her. But what could she do? If she took Daddy back his money, she would be married to William before the summer ended. Her life would be a living hell. She closed her eyes and fantasized about a life with Jackson instead.

Her fantasy didn't last. Once he found out the truth, he would kick her out on the street or worse.

Maryanne got up and paced. What if she stole a horse from Jackson and went east? It wasn't her destination of choice, but then putting Jackson at risk hadn't been either. She would never see him again, but she would be free.

Maryanne stumbled. Men frightened her. William told her all men had desires, and a woman's job was to satisfy them. Thoughts of a man touching her sent shivers down her back. She stopped. Unless the man was Jackson. She felt safe and cherished when he held her. Maryanne sat down on the edge of her bed. Once he discovered what she did, he would hate her. She wouldn't be able to look him in the eye, knowing how he felt about liars and thieves, and she was both.

There had to be another way. She could catch a ride into the next town and steal a horse there. She contemplated the idea and then threw it out too. It didn't matter where she went or what she did. She would be unable to bear Jackson's contempt. Maryanne laid there for hours wrestling with her conscience. In the end, she realized to make things right, she had to turn herself in. In jail, William couldn't hurt her, and Jackson would not be guilty of harboring a criminal.

Maryanne didn't see Jackson again until noon. He popped in long enough to hand her a tray, and then he left. Maryanne stared at the closed door. She felt like a criminal waiting for the hangman. With her, she wouldn't know when it was her last supper.

Maryanne looked out the window in her room. Wylder went on living despite the mess she made of her life. Wagons drove by loaded with goods from the rail station. Men on horses went about their business. Women and children walked back and forth across the streets. Maryanne let the calico curtains fall back into place. She missed Jackson and the talks they had while they shared their dinner. The noise of the busy livery filtered through the thin walls of her room. Was he with a customer, or avoiding her?

The memory of his kiss sparked in her mind. She remembered how his arms felt around her and the solid heat of his chest. She thought of the way his lips felt sliding along hers and how his tongue stroked hers. Maryanne walked back and forth. He liked her. He said as much before he told her there would be no more kissing. She knew she surprised him with her kiss. He must have been shocked by her brazen behavior. To be honest, she shocked herself. Jackson must think her without morals.

He said she belonged to William. She didn't, though. Maryanne was old enough to make her own decisions, and William would never be her husband. She would fight marriage to him with her dying breath. He was a cruel man, incapable of loving anyone more than his own lusts. He lived to serve his own pleasure.

When they were young, he didn't just pull her hair and tease her with frogs and bugs. He tied her down and cut her with his knife. The cuts weren't deep enough to draw attention. Just painful enough to make her obedient to his whims. Maryanne lived in terror of being alone with him. One time he caught a scorpion and cut off its tail. He used the stinger to force her into all kinds of things. She stole money from Mr. Smythe's desk, lied to Mrs. Smythe about William's whereabouts, and talked one of the Smythe's' housemaids into getting undressed with the door ajar so William could watch. He was ten at the time, and she just turned eight. Once they were older, William moved on to raping the housemaids and cutting numbers into their flesh. He wanted them to remember what number they were in his long line of offenses.

William threatened to kill Papa if Maryanne told him what he did to her. As a terrified little girl, Maryanne believed he would. As a grown woman of nineteen, she knew he could not. He could hire somebody and hope they didn't trace the crime back to him, but that was about it.

Maryanne sighed. She never knew a man like Jackson existed. She assumed they were variations of William and her father. Now she understood the difference, and she wanted more. She wanted Jackson, and she wanted every minute she could be with him. She had today. Who knew what tomorrow would bring?

Maryanne glanced out the window. If she hurried, she could make Jackson some soup like she planned the night William showed up in the livery and questioned Tom.

The noise died down, and Maryanne peeked out her door. The livery was empty. She slipped out of her room and closed the door behind her. She walked along the wall containing Jackson's door, as well as her own. Taking a deep breath to bolster her courage, Maryanne knocked and waited. When no one answered, she opened his door and peeked inside. Jackson wasn't there. She stepped through the door and closed it behind her. She stood in a small kitchen. A wood-burning stove stood to her left. A row of wooden shelves lined the wall next to it. Pans hung from hooks and tins lined the shelves. A wooden cabinet faced her. Dishpans rested on top of it beneath a window with yellow floral curtains. A wooden table sat in the center of the room, surrounded by four high-backed wooden chairs.

A large flour barrel sat beside the cabinet in front

of the window, and a fireplace filled the wall off to her right. She gazed at the cozy room. Maryanne had not looked around much when she visited before. She had been too busy watching Jackson.

Maryanne noticed a door beside the fireplace. It must lead to Jackson's bedroom. It stood ajar. She had only been in the small kitchen area. Curiosity got the better of her. She tip-toed across the wooden slat floor and peeked around the door. A large four-poster bed stood in the center of the room, covered with a multicolored patchwork quilt. Blue gingham curtains hung in front of a window, and Jackson's shirts hung from pegs beneath it. A fireplace burned off to her right. The room smelled like Jackson. Maryanne's stomach hitched. He was such a handsome man. She wondered why some woman hadn't snagged him before now.

Maryanne frowned at the thought. She wanted to snag him, but it would never happen. He would make someone else a good husband. He was kind, a gentleman, and he was clean. Maryanne's eyes widened as she realized how true the thought was. He had everything organized and in its place.

She returned to the main room. Her gaze fell on the row of pans beside the stove. She would make the best soup Jackson ever ate. How hard could it be? She was an intelligent woman. She could figure it out. And she watched Jackson several times.

Maryanne opened the cabinet doors and found a few potatoes and carrots. She found salt pork wrapped in cloth. She set the items on the cabinet. Jackson liked soup. He confessed as much when he brought her lunch one day. Maryanne looked around and decided she would make him biscuits as well.

Two hours later, Maryanne stood back and surveyed the scene. The stove had been difficult to light. Once she got it figured out, she started on the soup. She had a hard time finding a knife to peel the potatoes with and ended up cutting herself. In desperation, she took a large knife and chopped the vegetables into tiny pieces. The peelings would have to remain. Time drifted on, and she was nowhere near ready to impress Jackson with her culinary efforts. The floor vibrated as the train came up the tracks. The train whistle blew, and the engines hissed as the three o'clock train departed She had two hours to dazzle Jackson. Maryanne pumped water into a large pot and set it on the stove. She added the vegetables and set a lid on top like Jackson did.

Maryanne wandered over to the shelves and found a cookbook. She looked up biscuits and rolled up her sleeves.

Chapter Seven

Later in the evening, Jackson trudged toward the livery. A landowner on the west end of town had a horse with an infected leg. It took him all afternoon to get the wound cleaned and bandaged. The thoroughbred had been skittish. Jackson rolled his aching shoulders. He had to hold the horse down while he disinfected the wound. The landowner and his trainer helped. They were small men, and the burden of the job rested on Jackson. Some days he wished he stayed in Boston. He picked up a shipment of turpentine and belladonna at the rail office. He walked east down Old Cheyenne Road toward the livery. Old Cheyenne Road ran east and west through Wylder in front of the telegraph office, the stagecoach line, and the train depot. The wooden structures of the glassblower and the wagon repair shop were off to this left. As he neared the building, someone cried out. Jackson stopped in his tracks. A moan and a cough came next.

"Help me," a voice cried out. "Someone, help me."

Jackson walked toward the voice. "Where are you?" He searched the front of the wagon repair shop and walked around the east side.

"Here."

Jackson came across the slight form of a woman. She was one of the new immigrants new in town. A pretty little Irish girl he'd seen asking for work at the mercantile. She had red hair and blue eyes. She couldn't be more than eighteen years of age. She lay on the ground curled in a ball and shaking like a sapling in a windstorm. Blood covered her everywhere. Jackson hurried toward her and knelt at her side to estimate the damage.

"What's your name?" he asked as he surveyed her face. She had a gash on her cheek, and her eye was swollen shut. Her rapid breathing and pale, clammy skin told him she was in shock. He did a quick search for other wounds. His mouth tightened over her torn, bloody skirt. "Who did this to you?"

She shook her head. "I don't know his name." Her trembling increased. "He said he would pay me to do some laundry and mending for him." She bit her lip. "I never would've gone to the hotel with him if I'd known he would…" A spasm took hold of her. She trembled , moaning with pain.

Jackson looked around. He had nothing to cover her up with. He noticed blood pooling beneath her. "Where are you bleeding?"

"Where aren't I?" she replied. Her words broke off. She bent her head and whimpered with pain. Sobs shook her body.

Jackson noted the pallor of her face. "We need to get you to Doc Sullivan." He set his package against the side of the building and scooped the girl up in his arms.

She lifted her head. "Snake ring," she murmured and went limp in his arms. Her head hung awkwardly against him. Jackson shifted her, so her head rested against his chest. He strode toward Doc Sullivan's office. He walked north down the side street toward Wylder Street. He passed the church and the bank.

Everyone had gone home for the night.

The sheriff's office faced him. Sheriff Wylder stood on the wooden walkway outside. In his thirties with dark hair and a mustache, Branch Wylder wore his pistols low on his hips. He had an attitude with bad guys. "What you got there, Jackson?"

Jackson told him all he knew as he strode toward the doctor's office.

Branch Wylder fell into step beside him. "Let's see what the doc has to say about her." They passed the apothecary and Wylder Bakery. The sheriff tapped on the doctor's door and then swung it open for Jackson.

"Doc, we need you!" the sheriff shouted as he closed the door behind them.

An hour later, Jackson stood outside the doctor's office and let the cool of the evening blow on his face. The little Irish girl had been raped several times and beaten. She had several large lacerations down her arms and legs. The punctured lung created the real problem. She wouldn't live to see the dawn. Jackson shook his head.

Sheriff Wylder stepped out on the walkway beside him. "I think we have ourselves a murder."

"She said a man told her he had laundry and mending for her. She went with him to his hotel."

"Did she give any description?" the sheriff asked.

"No. The last thing she said was 'snake ring.'" Jackson stared down the street toward the wagon repair shop. "What kind of man would do such a thing?"

"Men. I'm thinking there were more than one from the extent of the damage." Sheriff Wylder checked his guns. "Poor girl has no family, so there's no one to notify." He paused. "I'll check into the strangers in town." He shook his head. "First there was the fellow shot in the back, then the bank robbery in Lonetree, and now this. Makes you wonder who we're dealing with."

Jackson agreed. The men in Wylder were decent. The strangers riding through got a little rough, but nothing like this ever happened before.

"I'll see you tomorrow," the sheriff said as he walked back toward his office.

Jackson waved and returned the way he came. Locusts hummed in the quiet of the evening. The pungent scent of sagebrush hung on the breeze. Jackson shook his head to erase the scenes he witnessed in the doctor's office. Somewhere out there an animal masqueraded as a man. He deserved to be put down. Jackson stopped. Maryanne's words floated through his mind. *Some men deserve to be shot in the back.* He had to admit, if he came across someone mistreating a woman the way the Irish girl had been he'd d shoot the man in the back, too. It wouldn't matter where she came from. Every woman deserved protection from a man who abused them.

Maryanne was alone at the livery. He quickened his step. The murdering bastards were out there somewhere.

Jackson retrieved his package from the wagon repair shop and headed for his livery. His stomach churned with the scenes he witnessed and anxiety for Maryanne.

"Anything happen while I was out?" he asked Tom as he walked toward his rooms.

Tom shook his head. "Not a thing. It's been pretty quiet."

Jackson nodded. Quiet was the reason he liked

Wylder. Most of the time. He stopped outside Maryanne's door and hesitated for several seconds. He didn't want to frighten her. The conversation he wanted to have with her would take a while. She saw something the night she got shot. Their kiss flashed through his mind. It shouldn't have happened. She tasted like honey, and he wanted more. The problem was her fiancé. Maryanne was spoken for. Jackson's stomach tightened. She didn't want the man and didn't agree to the marriage. She deserved better. Someone who understood how special she was. He never knew a woman with such a tender heart. She worried over every scratch she saw on him and paced the floor when he was late. She asked after his day and listened when he spoke of the difficulties he encountered. He looked forward to the time they spent together. Even his cat slept beside her fire.

Jackson stepped away from her door and walked toward his rooms. Maybe he should have a bath and clean up before he spoke to her. He smelled like horses and sweat. He strolled toward his rooms and stopped a few feet away. Curls of smoke rolled out into the livery from under his door. What the hell? He leaped toward the door, threw it open, and skidded to a stop.

Maryanne stood in the center of the room in a pink dress, covered with flour. He stared at the wisps of blonde hair plastered to her face. She had flour on her nose and cheeks. Her lips were red, and her face shone with perspiration. Lord, she was pretty.

He tore his gaze from her when the stove popped. Flames rose from a pan sitting on top. His gaze roamed the room. A pile of white sticky goo dripped from the table to the floor. Pans and tins were opened everywhere. Flour littered the floor, and God knew what else. Jackson looked from the floor, back to Maryanne, and over to the stove. He rushed into the room and slammed the door shut behind him. He grabbed the baking soda from the shelf, popped the lid off, and sprinkled the contents all over the top of the stove. The fire died and disappeared in a cloud of smoke. He gazed at the stove. The frying pan held an odd-shaped piece of charcoal. It smelled like burnt flesh. Jackson turned to Maryanne. Her eyes were wide as she stared at him.

"What's going on?" he asked in a casual tone. It could be a lot worse. He preferred a burnt dinner to the scenario he encountered earlier.

She blinked. "I wanted to…Well, I tried to make you some dinner." She held a large spoon. Her hands were covered with the same white sticky mess dripping from his table to the floor.

"I see," he managed to say. He looked the kitchen over. His spotless organized room looked like a tornado blew through.

Maryanne's face flushed. "I wanted to do something for you, to repay you for taking me in." She waved her hand at the kitchen. "I had one or two setbacks."

He glanced around the room. A rooster emerged from behind the table and pecked at what looked like vegetable pieces on the floor.

Jackson's eyebrow rose. "Is he part of your dinner plans? Or is he one of the setbacks?"

Maryanne looked from Jackson's face to the rooster. She flushed a bright red. "I didn't know he came in. I went to empty the pot out by the woodpile.

He must've followed me when I opened the door."

Jackson's lips twitched. "I'll take care of him."

She looked miserable. He wanted to laugh but didn't dare. He caught the rooster by the legs and took him outside. Maryanne was a sight. He couldn't get the image of her flour-dusted face from his mind. Cooking was not her forte.

He had a good chuckle and walked back inside. Maryanne stood beside the table, scraping the sticky mass into the chicken pail. She kept her head down and wouldn't look at him.

Jackson rolled up his sleeves. "Did my stove give you a hard time?" he asked as he pumped water into a pot and set it on the stove.

"Among other things," she answered.

"I can clean up here and go get us some dinner from the hotel."

Maryanne looked up. She blushed and waved her arms at his kitchen. "I'm sorry. I hoped to surprise you."

Jackson chuckled. "I am surprised."

"Not in a good way. I wanted to do something for you, and instead"—she waved her arms around again.—"all this happened." She looked close to tears.

Jackson walked toward her. She sure was pretty when she dressed like a girl. Her blue eyes gazed up at him. Pink touched her cheeks, and her lips parted as he approached. Her blonde hair shone in the dimming light.

"What were you trying to make?" he asked with a straight face.

She dropped her gaze. "Soup and biscuits."

Jackson stopped in front of her. "Have you ever

cooked before?"

Maryanne flushed again. "No, but I watched a few times."

Jackson nodded. "Let's clean up, and I'll give you your first lesson."

Maryanne looked around the room and nodded. "Okay."

An hour and a half later, they sat at the wooden table and sipped the steaming soup in their bowls.

They put the kitchen in order, and a fire burned bright in the hearth.

The soup was delicious. Maryanne said as much. "How do you know how to cook?"

Jackson shrugged. "I've lived on my own since I turned eighteen. I got tired of eating in public houses and learned to do for myself."

****

Maryanne shook her head in amazement. Her body still trembled from Jackson's closeness as he showed her how to peel the vegetables. He stood behind her with his arms on either side of her. He held her hands and showed her the proper movement to make. "Always cut away from your body," he said. His deep voice rumbled behind her head. She dared not breathe. His large, muscular body surrounded her. She resisted the urge to lean back against him.

He was a patient man. She made a mess of his kitchen, and he said nothing. She burned the salt pork and the soup. The rooms smelled of it. Jackson opened the windows and let the breeze air the room out while they wiped down every surface in the kitchen and washed the dishes. She had no idea how the rooster got in. Jackson took care of him, too.

Jackson was kind, and a gentleman. Maryanne studied him. Why couldn't Papa want her to marry someone like Jackson? A wealthy family name and a college education did not create a man worth knowing. William would never be Jackson's equal. They been alone in Jackson's rooms for several hours, and not once had he been inappropriate. William would have. He liked to make her uncomfortable.

They spent the time they cleaned and made dinner talking. He told her about his practice in Boston and some of the amusing things he encountered. Maryanne talked about her home and her horse. She avoided any topic which might give her identity away.

When they wiped the last dish and returned it to the shelf, they shared a comfortable silence. She loved sitting here in Jackson's kitchen and watching the fire flicker. Security, warmth, and love created a home. Jackson and his kitchen held it all. Maryanne sighed. "Thank you for everything you've done for me."

Jackson's hazel eyes roamed her face. "You're welcome." He paused. "I've been searching for the right words to tell you something. I'm afraid there is no easy way." He took a deep breath. "I found a woman on my way home tonight."

Maryanne's head shot up. "Excuse me?"

Jackson shook his head. "She was beaten and bloody." He hesitated. "I know you saw something the night you were shot. They tried to shoot you in the back, and Mr. Conway ended up dead." He shook his head. "Nothing like this has ever happened in Wylder before. You said you came across a group of men. I think one of them is in town."

"I think so, too," Maryanne answered. William

was. One or more of his friends might be, also. Her heart rose to her throat. "How is she?"

Jackson shook his head. "She'll be dead before morning." He rose to his feet. "Is there anything you can tell me about the night you were shot?"

Maryanne swallowed. "No." She would burn in hell for the lies she told, but she wanted to do this on her own terms. She would turn herself in, not wait until Sheriff Wylder came for her. The less Jackson knew, the better. He could say he had no idea, and it would be the truth.

Jackson let his breath out. "Someone in Wylder raped and beat the Irish girl. She swooned before she gave us any details. I wonder if it's the same group of men you ran in to." Jackson walked toward Maryanne. "Until the bastards are caught, you need to stay out of sight."

Maryanne agreed. But it wasn't a stranger who frightened her. It was William.

"Come on," Jackson said. "I'll walk you back to your room."

He opened the door for her. They walked the short distance in silence. Maryanne mused at the difference between Jackson and William. Both were large men. Both lived in large cities. William came from money. Jackson did not. Jackson spoke of his parents with affection. William hated his. Jackson was careful to be proper. William did not.

When they stood outside her door, Maryanne looked up at Jackson. He was such a handsome man. Her gaze wandered over his wavy brown hair and straight nose. She looked at his square chin and the intense green and gold of his eyes. They stared at each other. The silver light of the moon fell through the windows up above, silhouetting his large frame. Maryanne licked her lips. She stared at his mouth and wondered if he would kiss her. Jackson leaned close. His breath blew across her cheek. Maryanne trembled in anticipation. He gazed deep into her eyes. She held her breath and waited. His face hovered inches from hers. She closed her eyes.

The door behind her opened. "Have a good night, Maryanne. Get some rest. I'll check on you in the morning."

"Wait." She grasped his hand in both of hers and gazed up into his eyes. "Would you marry me if things were different?" She blurted it out and waited. Her heart thumped hard in her chest.

He remained silent for several agonizing seconds. "If what were different?" he asked. He searched her face. "I haven't thought about courting or women since I came to Wylder." He frowned.

"Oh." She flushed with embarrassment. Her mouth got her into more trouble. "Good night, then." she managed to whisper and turned away. She stepped inside her door and gazed back at him.

Jackson looked confused. "'Night." He answered, and then he disappeared.

Maryanne stood for some time, staring after him. Jackson didn't sound very enthused about having a wife. She hadn't wanted to be one until now. Why would he hurry into a new relationship after the way Caroline treated him? Jackson didn't know what Maryanne had done, or he would be less enthused. She knew what she had to do. If she waited until the sheriff figured it out or someone recognized her, Jackson would go to jail again. She would not be able to live with herself if that happened. She closed her door. First thing tomorrow, she would fix everything she ruined.

Chapter Eight

Maryanne woke to the smell of fire. She sat up, clutching her bedclothes to her chest. White fingers of smoke curled in from under her closed door. The horses were going crazy out in the livery. Boots ran past her door and men shouted. She slipped out of bed and pulled on her bathrobe. She tugged her boots on and hurried to her door. She touched the surface. It wasn't hot. Maryanne sighed with relief and peeked outside.

Chaos ruled the livery. Horses reared and kicked at the gates to their stalls. Jackson and his three men led them out the large double doors. Smoke filled the livery, making it difficult to see or breathe. Fire popped and crackled along the east wall. She threw an arm over her nose and mouth.

"Here, let me help you outside." Jackson stood beside her. His hands held a lead rope. A dozen more horses raced around their corrals, screaming in fright.

"I can't go out there," Maryanne protested.

"You can't stay in here, either" Jackson answered.

"What am I going to do?" Maryanne asked.

The black mare next to them reared and snorted. Jackson ran a hand through his hair. "It's dark outside, and half the town is out there in their nightshirts. No one will notice you unless you draw attention to yourself. They're too busy putting the fire out. Just keep your head down and stick to the shadows."

"Okay." Maryanne sagged against the door frame.

"I'll take you to a safe place." Jackson took her arm and helped her out of the livery and around by Dugan's Blacksmith shop. He was right. No one looked at them. Jackson left her by the side of the building. "Stay out of sight until I come back for you," he ordered. Then he left.

Maryanne surveyed the scene. Townspeople formed a line from the well in the yard to the east end of the livery, where the fire licked away at the side of the building. They passed wooden buckets of water and threw them on the fire. Smoke and steam rose in white sheets. The horses in the pen galloped around in circles. They were frightened and whinnied in discontent. Jackson came out with a large bay stallion and put him in the livery yard. He latched the gate shut. Then, he looked up and smiled in her direction. Maryanne ducked behind the corner of the corral. Her heart flipped over in her chest. She peeked out as he disappeared inside the livery stable. Her belly fluttered with excitement. He smiled for her and no one else. He wanted her to know he cared.

"Well, well, well," a voice said beside her.

Maryanne turned to stone. She knew his voice.

She turned around and faced her greatest nightmare, William Smythe.

"What do you want?" she croaked.

He leaned against the side of the building and studied her face. "I came looking for a murderer and find my fiancée." He looked her up and down. "I knew Mr. Daniels had a secret. No man is as innocent as he pretends to be." He took a step toward her. "What are you doing in Wylder? You should be in Lonetree."

Maryanne swallowed the fear rising in her throat. "I am not your fiancée, and I don't need your permission to be here. I can go where I like and do what I like." She lifted her chin in challenge.

Retribution came swift. He twisted her arm behind her back and shoved her into the side of the blacksmith shop. "It's time you learned to control your mouth. I don't like it when you challenge me, as you'll soon learn."

Her head swam and her arm burned. If he twisted any harder, it would break. She bit back her cry of pain. Her vision blurred, and she couldn't move.

William's breath blew hot against her cheek. "Apologize," he commanded as he pulled up on her twisted arm.

Tears spilled over and ran down her cheeks. Dizziness washed over her. Maryanne groaned. "I…am…sorry."

He pushed her one more time and then let go. He caught her arm and spun her to face him. She cried out. Her arm hung limp by her side. Pain raced up and down her wounded limb. William shook her hard.

Maryanne bit her lip. Her teeth chattered. "Let me go!"

He caught her chin and tilted her face up. "Don't ever speak to me like that again. I'll do whatever I like with you."

Maryanne trembled. She glanced around for Jackson but couldn't see him anywhere. "I'm not your property. Unhand me this instant."

"You're a woman and my intended. Both of which make you, my property." His gaze narrowed on her face. "Are you looking for Mr. Daniels? He won't be able to help you."

Maryanne refused to meet his eyes.

William hit her in the face. "Look at me when I speak to you." The blurry image of William danced before her. "We have unfinished business, you and I. You know something, and I will discover what it is." He glanced around. "Our discussion will have to wait for a more private setting. I'll be back." He stepped closer to whisper in her ear. "Don't tell the overgrown farmer I'm here. I have a surprise for him. He'll pay for touching my property." He punched her in the stomach before turning away. Maryanne wilted against the side of the building. She wanted to yell she wasn't his property, but she didn't have any air in her lungs.

The next thing she knew, she lay on the ground with Jackson walking toward her. The look on his face sent chills down her spine.

****

Jackson walked through the double doors of the livery. Two more horses needed to be rescued, and then they could help with the fire. Jackson gazed around. Smoke billowed from the back of the livery.

"You go," Tom called. "We got the last two."

Jackson nodded. Tom and Hank, one of his other hands, entered the stalls of the last two horses.

Jackson hurried toward Maryanne's door and looked inside. Smoke curled around the window. He frowned. The fire must have circled to the back of the building. She would need her things. He glanced around. Jackson grabbed Maryanne's dresses off the pegs and stuffed them inside her valise. He turned to go and remembered her saddlebags. He crouched beside the bed and pulled them forward. The leather strap gave way, and the contents spilled out onto the floor. Jackson froze. Paper bills and gold coins filled the bag. He lifted the saddlebags onto the bed and checked the other side. It contained the same. He reeled with disbelief. What the hell had Maryanne gotten herself into?

He couldn't believe his eyes. He stared for several minutes and then drew the flap over the money and did up both straps. Anger surged through him and his hands shook. Jackson sucked in a deep breath. *Déjà vu* rocked him to the souls of his boots. His past rose and crashed over him with the force of a tsunami. He relived the incident in Boston, where he faced prosecution for a crime he didn't commit. And all because he helped a lady in distress. Would he never learn? Jackson swore and kicked the straight-back chair. Old emotions he thought long buried rose in his chest. He wanted to punch a hole in the wall but restrained himself. He didn't have the money nor the time to fix it. He stared at the saddlebags for long minutes, then slid them back beneath Maryanne's bed.

A knock sounded on the door. "Jackson, we got all the horses, and the men say the fire is out," Tom called.

Jackson looked toward the door. "Okay. I'll be right there." The smoke curling in her window must have come from the last of the fire as it died out.

A picture of Maryanne flashed through his mind. The way she'd been when he found her in his rooms making him dinner. with her pink dress covered in flour, and her hair falling around her flushed face. Who was she? He didn't even know her real name. He knew Maryanne Jones wasn't it. If the fire was out, Maryanne's things weren't in danger. He set her valise on the stiff-backed chair and strode from the room.

Why would her saddlebags be full of money? Did she rob the bank in Lonetree or take it from the men who did? What the hell happened that night? Who were the men? Who shot Rex Conway? What connection did she have with him, and where did he fit into this mess?

Jackson shook his head. Maryanne had intelligence and a good sense of humor, but it was obvious she had a side to her he didn't know. To think he almost fell for her big blue eyes and innocent expression. He believed her story about running away from her father. That much rang true. As for the rest, he wanted answers.

He walked outside and around to Dugan's Blacksmith shop and stopped short. His heart dropped to the heels of his boots. Maryanne lay on the ground beside the wooden building. She blinked her beautiful eyes at him and then passed out.

****

Maryanne woke up with a start. She hit the hands that soothed her. Something wet and cold pressed against her left eye. "Go away! I never want to see you again!"

"Who?" Jackson's deep voice vibrated by her ear.

She opened her eyes.

He sat beside her with a damp cloth in his hand. He looked at her with one eyebrow quirked. "You don't want to see who again?"

Maryanne blinked. One eye was swollen shut. She lay in her bed in the pale green room. Morning sunshine poured in through her window. Silence filled the space between them as he waited for her answer. They were alone. She took a deep breath to calm the flutter in her heart. "No one." She smiled up at him. "I had a bad dream."

Jackson didn't smile back. "Who hit you?" He gazed deep into her eyes when he asked the question.

Maryanne frowned. "No one." Lying to Jackson was the hardest thing she ever did.

"Then how did you get the black eye?" Jackson asked, leaning toward her. His face gave nothing of his thoughts away.

Maryanne grimaced. "I tripped in the dark."

Jackson looked at her for long moments. Disappointment shone from his beautiful hazel eyes. "I thought we were past the part where we lied to each other. I guess we're not." He got up and walked to the fireplace. "I want the truth." He frowned. "Is Maryanne even your name?"

Maryanne hung her head. She wanted to tell him. But how did she say, "Hey, I know you don't like thieves, but I robbed my father's bank because he wouldn't listen to me?" Or "Hey, you know the dandy who came in here asking questions? He is my fiancé. He likes to rape women and beat them up."

Jackson stared into the empty hearth. "I have work to do. The men are waiting on me." He turned his head and speared her with his glare. "I'll give you until sundown. You know where to find me when you're ready to talk."

She nodded her head.

He went out, closing the door behind him.

Maryanne rolled to her side and curled up. The look in Jackson's eyes would haunt her for the rest of her life. It was all her fault. Every bit of it. Jackson had been nothing but kind. He offered her a place to stay and stitched her up. He sheltered and protected her while she healed. He was a good man and deserved better. She stared at her valise on the high-backed chair. She could leave. Jackson wouldn't stand in her way. Tears gathered in her eyes. She could go wherever she wanted. She had the money right there in her saddlebags. The one thing stopping her was her injury. Maryanne squeezed her eyes shut. And Jackson.

She couldn't bear the disappointment in his gaze. She'd let him down, and if she didn't do something quick, he would lose everything again.

Then there was William. His voice spoke in her head. *"We have unfinished business, you and I. You know something, and I will discover what it is...Our discussion will have to wait for a more private setting. I'll be back."* His kind of talks involved a lot of pain. Hers.

Maryanne got up and went to the window. Some of the men in town were helping Jackson repair the fire damage. She could hear them laughing while they worked. Jackson's deep laugh echoed through the building. She wrapped her arms around her middle. She wished his laughter could be part of her life forever. Would he want her if things were different? She relived their kiss in her mind. Jackson made her feel things she never dreamed she would. He changed her. She no longer wanted to travel to California or the Orient. She wanted to stay here with Jackson. She wanted to live in Wylder as Jackson's wife. They would build a life together, have children, and grow old. Maryanne wiped the tears from her cheeks. She didn't panic when she thought of making children with Jackson. He would be gentle. She knew it in her heart. Jackson was honest, dependable, and the kind of man every woman dreamed about. But she knew the truth. Jackson would never be hers.

Maryanne let the curtains fall back into place. She wondered if her father noticed she hadn't returned. With a sigh, Maryanne laid down. Apart from her swollen eye, she was well enough to travel. She determined to set it all right. Then the fire happened.

Maryanne limped over to her bed. She had to make it right. Jackson deserved the truth. And there was no time like the present.

She noticed her dresses were not on the pegs anymore but stuffed inside her valise. She pulled out a dark blue calico and clean undergarments. Maryanne took a deep breath and tugged her nightgown over her head. After her talk with Jackson, she would go find the sheriff.

When she buttoned her last button, Maryanne brushed out her hair and plaited it down her back. No sense in making it pretty. No one would notice anyway. She took her clothes out and refolded them, so they were tidy. Then she made the bed. She dreaded the talk she knew she had to have, but there was no use putting it off any longer. Taking a deep breath and stiffening her spine, Maryanne opened her door and stepped out into the livery.

Tom and another man were pitching hay. The other man was in his early twenties with blond hair and green eyes. He stopped dead when he spotted Maryanne and whistled beneath his breath.

Tom turned around and froze. "Can we help you, miss?"

Maryanne walked toward them. "I'm looking for Jackson."

Tom smiled. "He's around the east side of the

corrals fixing the fence."

Maryanne nodded. She made her way through the double doors and out into the heat of the Wyoming sun. It took her eyes a minute or two to adjust. She walked toward the east corner and rounded it in time to see Jackson smile at a pretty little woman with long white-blonde hair. Maryanne stopped dead in her tracks. She had no right to be jealous. Jackson wouldn't want anything to do with her once he knew what she did.

Maryanne made her way over to them. The men working on the corral fence gazed at her with open curiosity. The woman with the long white-blonde hair turned when Maryanne approached.

Jackson looked up. His smile disappeared when he made eye contact.

The woman looked from Jackson to her and back. She stuck her hand out. "Hello, I'm Cissy Standish."

Maryanne shook her hand. "My name is Maryanne."

Cissy smiled. "It's nice to meet you. Are you a friend of Jackson's?" she asked.

Maryanne glanced at Jackson. "I'm not sure." She smiled at Cissy and turned to Jackson. "I'm ready to talk to you."

Jackson removed his hat and wiped the perspiration from his brow. "This better be good."

Maryanne's spirits plummeted. He wouldn't make it easy for her. She stood in awkward silence beside them, thinking of what to say. She couldn't bear the cold look in Jackson's eyes.

"You go ahead, Jackson. We got this." The man beside Jackson rose to his feet. Tall and lean with long dark hair, the man smiled at her.

"You sure?" Jackson asked.

"I'm sure." The man held his hand out to Maryanne. "I'm Buck Standish, part-owner of this livery and Jackson's partner."

Maryanne shook his hand. So this was the famous gun for hire turned citizen. He turned his life around. There might be hope for her after all.

Maryanne smiled. "It's very nice to meet you."

Jackson grabbed her arm and turned her around. They walked back the way she came in silence.

He led her past the livery toward the train tracks. "Well?" he asked. "Let's hear it."

Maryanne stopped. Now the moment arrived, she lost her nerve. She clasped her hands together to hide their shaking and lifted her gaze to his face. "My name is Maryanne Wagner. I robbed the bank in Lonetree."

Chapter Nine

"I know," Jackson said.

Maryanne gaped at him. "How?" she asked.

Jackson shrugged. "I went to rescue your belongings. Your saddlebag tipped over, and the money fell out." He studied Maryanne's face.

She went pale. "My father is Phineas Wagner, President of Wagner Trust of Lonetree."

"I figured you came from money. There aren't a lot of women out here who don't cook or sew. Those who don't know how had servants to do the chores for them." His tone was flat. So were his eyes.

Maryanne twisted her fingers together, not sure how to take his comment. So she ignored it. "I meant to tell you."

Jackson didn't answer. His gazed into the distance with his hands on his hips and waited for her to say more.

She explained about the bank and the deal her father made with Bernard Smythe. Jackson stood impassive. He wouldn't look at her.

"I never meant to hurt anyone. I wanted my father to realize I was serious about William Smythe. I'll never agree to marry him!"

"William Smythe is your fiancé?" If anything, the knowledge made him angrier.

Maryanne nodded.

"So, he came looking for you." Jackson's tone remained flat and emotionless.

"No. He came looking for the person who shot Rex. He didn't know about me until last night." She willed him to look at her. When he did, she took a step back.

Fury shot from his eyes. "Who hit you last night?" He ran his hands through his hair. "I'm not sure I believe anything you say. You lied to me."

Maryanne swallowed. "I had to. If you knew what William was like, you'd understand why."

Jackson glared. "Nothing is so bad you can't tell the truth. I thought we had something going, you and me. I thought you were different. I thought you were special." He turned back toward the tracks. "I was wrong."

Pain seared her heart. "We do have something special."

"Not if you can sit on a case of money, you robbed and lie about your name. What makes it unforgivable is you know about Boston and my past. You put me, the livery, and everybody connected to it in danger." He turned to her again. "Have you told me everything, or is there more? Did you know Rex Conway? "

Maryanne dropped her head. "He's William's friend." She took a deep breath, preparing herself to tell him the rest of it.

"Do you know who shot him?" Jackson asked.

"Yes," Maryanne answered. "Please look at me. I want to tell you what happened. I want to explain…"

"There isn't anything to explain. You're not the woman I thought you were."

Agony tore her heart to shreds. "I have a good

reason. Let me explain, you'll see I had no choice."

"There is always a choice," he answered.

Maryanne wiped the tears from her cheeks. "I want to put it right, Jackson. I want to make it up to you. I never meant to involve you or any of the people in Wylder. This is my battle. I will be the one to fight it." Her voice quivered.

Jackson didn't look at her. "Go, fight it then. I'm not stopping you."

Maryanne stared at his profile. His face could have been carved in stone. She touched his sleeve, hoping he would relent.

He turned away.

"I'm sorry, Jackson, whether you believe it or not. I never meant to involve anyone else in my mess." She turned and walked away. Tears blurred her vision. Her heart shattered into a million pieces and kept on breaking with every step she took. There would never be another man like him. Not for her.

She hurried toward the livery, oblivious to the curious stares of the townspeople. Once inside, she penned a note to Jackson, explaining all the things she couldn't say to his face. She set it on the bed and gathered up her saddlebags. She slung them across her good shoulder and looked at her valise. The saddlebags would slow her down. She wouldn't be able to walk to the sheriff's office with both. Her valise would have to stay. She wouldn't need it in jail. With a sigh of resignation, Maryanne set her valise on the wooden bench and squared her shoulders. Best get this thing over with.

She walked out of the livery and turned west. She didn't want to face Jackson and the men working on the east side of the building. She had enough hostility for one day. Once she cleared the livery and the blacksmith shop, she walked north down the backstreet. The saddlebags wore on her shoulder with their weight. She put her head down and hitched her shoulder to redistribute the weight. She didn't see the man on the boardwalk step on his cigarette and walk toward her until it was too late.

"What have you got there?"

Her heart plummeted. Panic tightened her chest. Of course, she would run into William while she tried to make things right with Jackson. She looked up in time to see the sheriff trot down the street on his horse. She would get no help there. He was too far away to hear her call. Fear caused her to trip. Maryanne kept her head down and kept walking. If she could get away from William, she would sit in the sheriff's office and wait for him. She hoped to reach Wylder Street before William got physical with her. She didn't make it.

He grabbed her arm and swung her around to face him. The saddlebags slipped from her shoulder and fell to the ground spilling open.

Maryanne dropped down and scooped bundles of bills and coins back into the bag. William caught her hand. "Well, well, what have we got here?" He lifted the flap and peered inside. His surprised expression would have been comical if it weren't so serious. He gave her a calculated stare. "You robbed your father's bank?" He rose to his feet and laughed aloud. "Here, I've been arguing with the old man to give me some money, and you had all of this."

Maryanne looked right and left. There had to be a way to escape. People walked by on the boardwalk, looking at them with curiosity. Jackson would hear of this before too long. If she didn't turn herself in, he'd think she ran away. He seemed convinced she took after Abigail O'Conner, willing to let someone else take the blame. She would prove him wrong by taking the money back and confessing. William would ruin all of it. Maryanne stepped back. He wouldn't hit her while they had an audience, but she didn't want to tempt fate, either. "I'm giving it to the sheriff. Get out of my way."

William's eyebrow rose. He narrowed his gaze in warning. "I see you haven't learned who is boss yet. You're challenging me, again. Apologize."

Fear tightened her stomach. "I will not. Now move."

Rage twisted his features. He glanced around at the people walking in and out of the bank and plastered a polite smile on his face. "If you confess, the sheriff will arrest you."

Maryanne shrugged. "If I'm in jail, I won't have to marry you. It seems like a rather good trade to me."

William's smile scared the hell out of her. "I think you're forgetting my father's lawyers and their ability to get charges dropped." He stroked her cheek with a gentle finger and smiled at the ladies walking past so they would think nothing of the encounter. "I also think you are underestimating your father's need for the loan my father gave him. The money you stole." He laughed. "I never would have believed it if I didn't see it with my own eyes." Then he sobered. His gaze turned cold. "My father made marrying you a condition to receive any more funds from him, the bastard." William spit into the dirt at their feet.

"I would rather die," Maryanne said emphatically.

William shrugged. "I like my life the way it is, but I do need a source of revenue. It occurs to me there is a solution to both our problems. I'll relieve you of those saddlebags, and I'll kill you. It's a winning solution. Everyone is happy, and we both get what we want. The problem is your attitude. I can't overlook the insubordination you're exhibiting. I warned you never to speak to me so disrespectfully again. For punishment, I'm going to turn you over to Porter and James before I slit your throat. They both have a hankering for virgins." He smiled and tipped his hat at another passerby.

Maryanne's blood froze in her veins. Panic covered her in a fine sheen. Her mind refused to think past her need to escape. She looked toward Wylder Street and wondered if she could make it before William caught her. She couldn't allow him to take the money, and she wouldn't let him kill her. Terror heightened her senses.

Thinking fast, she screamed as loud as she could and bent over to grab her saddlebags from the ground. Her sudden movement caught William off guard. When she came up, she lifted her knee hard into William's groin. He bent over with a curse and grabbed for her, howling with pain. Maryanne was ready. She turned and swung the saddlebags around as hard as she could and whacked him in the head. He dropped to the ground unconscious. Men and women came running over.

"Are you all right, miss?" one man asked.

"Yes," she said breathlessly. "This man tried to take my saddlebags from me. They have everything I own in this world." She didn't have to pretend to be frightened. Terror turned her blood ice cold.

"Of all the nerve," one woman said. "You go on,

honey. We'll make sure this man doesn't follow you."

Maryanne nodded and hurried away. For the first time in her life, she thanked God for making her female.

The people crowded around to get a look at William. They gossiped among themselves over the situation.

Maryanne crossed Wylder Street and hustled into the sheriff's office. She couldn't turn herself in now. What William said was true. Her father wanted the money and marrying her to William had been part of the deal. It wouldn't matter what charges were brought against her. She'd be out of jail and handed over to William with a gift bow before she could say, "I'd rather die."

She found a piece of paper and ink on the sheriff's desk and wrote her confession for the bank robbery. She set the saddlebags on the floor where the sheriff would see them and put her note on top.

Maryanne stopped.

In order to disappear where nobody could find her, she would need money. With a grimace of distaste, she took out a bundle of bills and tucked them into the pocket of her dress. She closed the flap once more and replaced the note. She'd make sure she paid her father back for the bundle and the hundred dollars she gave to Sadie. Maryanne slid the sheriff's chair in front of the saddlebags so any interested party wouldn't see them.

She peeked out of the door. The crowd still milled around William. Someone called for the doctor. Maryanne walked past them all and ran back to the livery. She slipped into her room and grabbed her valise. Any minute now, William could regain consciousness and come looking for her.

She frowned. If she changed into the men's clothing, she could disappear without unwanted attention. Maryanne trembled. She didn't have time to change. The three o'clock train to Laramie would leave any minute now. If she hurried, she could catch it. Maryanne grabbed her valise and ran down Old Cheyenne Road to the train depot. Two people were in front of her purchasing tickets. She stood on one foot and the other keeping a lookout for William and his friends. Her breath caught when the sheriff rode past on his horse. He paid no attention to her. He stopped to speak to the conductor.

"Can I help you, miss?" the ticket master asked.

Maryanne blew a sigh of relief and bought a one-way ticket to Laramie. She boarded the train and picked the car with the most passengers. She wanted a crowd in case William caught her before she got away.

The train whistle blew.

"All aboard," the conductor called.

Maryanne glanced at the window. There was no sign of William, Porter, or James. She closed her eyes with relief. The train whistle blew again, and the steam engine hissed. The train chugged forward.

Maryanne opened her eyes and glanced out the little window next to her seat. Jackson stood in the middle of the road. His hands were on his hips. Their gazes clashed as the train picked up speed. He would never forgive her. The anger in his expression settled in her stomach like a rock. She sat back with a sob. He must think her a coward. But she wasn't like Abigail O'Conner. Sure, she ran, but with good reason. She wished she could explain about William and the mess she made. Her note would have to do if he bothered to read it. She didn't fancy being locked up and at Mr. Smythe and her father's mercy. Who knew what plan they would concoct for her future?

Jackson's voice played in her head. *"Go, fight it then. I'm not stopping you."* She knew he would be angry. And with his history, how could he not? The tears began again. She would never see him again, nor would she return to Wylder. The conductor made his way through the passenger cars asking for tickets. Maryanne presented hers and waited while he punched it. She pulled her valise into her lap and hugged it to her chest as the conductor walked away. There was a finality about the disappearing town. She would never return, and it broke what remained of her heart. It shouldn't matter what Jackson thought. She would go far away and never come back. Rex's murder still hung over her head. She couldn't confess to shooting him either. If she did, same scenario. She'd be released into William's hands. Maryanne shivered to the toes of her shoes. She hoped they never figured out where she went.

****

Jackson woke before the sun and made himself a pot of coffee. He stood outside the livery and waited for the sun to appear on the horizon. It was his favorite time of day. The sky turned blue and pink as the light changed the night to day. Maryanne's tear-stained face flashed through his mind. Once he had a chance to calm down, he realized he never gave her the opportunity to tell her side of the story. Every time she tried, he cut her off. He went to find her when he learned a stranger attacked a woman in front of the bank. The man tried to take her saddlebags. Jackson's gut twisted. He remembered the face of the little Irish girl and his heart lodged in his throat. The man with the snake ring could still be in town. He might have found Maryanne. He rushed to the bank. Everyone was gone. The sheriff went looking for a stranger who came in on the train. Jackson retraced his steps and looked up as the Overland Express chugged away. Maryanne's pale face looked back. Where did she plan to go? She said it was her fight, and she planned to fight it. He wanted to catch her and tell her to come back. He wanted to know the name of the man who attacked her. He realized at the same time that she never told him who hit her last night during the fire. He got the sense she wouldn't be back. His heart dropped to his stomach. He knew the three o'clock train went to Laramie. He turned back to the livery. Tom hadn't come in today, and the night chores fell to him. First thing tomorrow, he would see if Buck could watch the livery so he could find Maryanne. They had unfinished business to sort through.

****

"Mornin'."

Jackson turned. Sheriff Wylder strolled toward him and stopped. "Morning," Jackson replied.

"You got any more coffee?" the sheriff asked.

Jackson nodded. "Yes, I do. Come on in, Sheriff." He turned and walked inside the livery and toward the back where his rooms were located.

The sheriff sat at his table and sipped the cup of coffee Jackson handed him. "I had a surprise waiting for me under my desk last night."

Jackson tipped his chair and waited.

"A pair of saddlebags filled with money."

Jackson sipped his coffee. "I heard."

"The saddle bags also contained a note addressed to me from Miss Maryanne Wagner of Lonetree. She confessed to the bank robbery in Lonetree and identified herself as the president of the bank's daughter."

Jackson nodded his head. He waited for the sheriff to continue. Buck should be here any minute so he could go.

"I sent a telegram to Sheriff Anderson last night informing him about the money and note. He sent word back this morning." Branch Wylder leaned back in his chair. "The sheriff said the robbery was an inside job. He also confirmed Mr. Wagner's daughter is missing."

Jackson sipped the black liquid in his cup and nodded. "Go on."

The sheriff swirled his cup, gazing into the depths. "The description he gave of the banker's daughter fits a girl several witnesses saw coming out of your livery."

Jackson sat his chair legs back on the floor. "That's right."

"I don't think Mr. Wagner plans to press charges against her. The sheriff said something about there being a family disagreement." Sheriff Wylder studied Jackson's face. "Is there anything you want to tell me, Jackson?"

Jackson rose to his feet. "I gave her a place to stay while she healed."

The sheriff finished off his coffee and set the cup on the table. "Why didn't you come to me?"

Jackson froze. "Come to you with what?"

"With the stolen money." Sheriff Wylder rose to his feet. "You knew she robbed the bank in Lonetree, and you let her hide out here to avoid the law. Mr. Smythe informs me the girl is his fiancée. He wants to press charges."

Jackson rubbed a hand over his face. "I didn't know who she was. I found her dressed as a boy in my stall. She told me men were looking for her to kill her." He explained everything to Sheriff Wylder.

The sheriff shook his head. "You should've told me, Jackson."

Jackson nodded. "I had no idea what her name was or what she did until yesterday. Maryanne made me promise to give her time to fix it."

Sheriff Wylder nodded. "Since her father isn't pressing charges, there is no reason to get worked up." He paused. "I told Mr. Smythe you hadn't broken any laws. He should take up any personal grievances with you." He paused. "One thing though, Sheriff Anderson wants you to bring the girl and the money to Lonetree."

Jackson froze. "Why me?"

"The sheriff said Miss Wagner must trust you to stay as long as she did in Wylder. If he or the girl's father comes, she'll bolt." He searched Jackson's face. "It's more than that, though, isn't it?"

"Yeah," Jackson answered.

"You care about her?"

Jackson nodded.

"Sheriff Anderson has a couple questions to ask you." He glanced around. "Where is the girl? Take me to her. I'd like to talk to her before she goes."

Jackson shook his head. "I can't do it. Miss Maryanne left yesterday afternoon on the train to Laramie. I can show you where she stayed." He led the sheriff to Maryanne's door. He hadn't been in here since their disagreement yesterday. Jackson opened the door and walked inside. Empty, silent, and immaculate, the room contained nothing to indicate Maryanne had been there except the scent of the room. It smelled like her.

He tugged in the scent and stilled. He missed her, and she had been gone one night. A folded note lay on the bed. He walked over and picked it up. His name jumped out at him from the top of the paper, written in delicate flowing letters. The paper smelled like her, too. He closed it and slid it into his shirt pocket.

"Do you know how long she plans to stay in Laramie?" the sheriff asked after opening drawers and poking around under the bed.

"No," Jackson said. "I think Laramie is a stopping-off point. I didn't get the feeling she planned to come back. I was angry when I found out about the money and told her to leave." He touched the note in his pocket. "I need to find her so we can work things out."

The sheriff walked toward the door. "I'll find her. You deliver the money to Sheriff Anderson and tell him where I went."

Jackson nodded. "Okay. I'm waiting for Buck. He'll look after the livery for me while I'm gone."

The sheriff turned to Jackson. "When I get back, I want you to tell me the whole story from the beginning."

Jackson nodded. He saddled his horse while he waited. He wished he would have let Maryanne explain. So much for promises and new beginnings.

Chapter Ten

Jackson rode for Lonetree with the saddlebags slung on behind him. He didn't want to take them to Sheriff Anderson, but he had no choice. They telegraphed the train depot in Laramie. No one with Maryanne's description bought a ticket. Next, they sent a telegram to the sheriff of Laramie. He had no information for them either. Maryanne disappeared without a trace. Sheriff Wylder left Deputy Wilson in charge and rode to Laramie to ask around.

When Jackson told Maryanne to go, he didn't think she would do it. She surprised him. Caroline would have pouted and forced him to apologize. Then she would have gotten revenge by going to dinner alone with someone he despised. Maryanne was unlike any woman he ever met. She wore men's breeches, robbed a bank, and couldn't cook. What other surprises did she have in store?

Jackson rode into Lonetree midafternoon, tired and ready for some food.

He rode down the main street to the sheriff's office on the east end of town.

Sheriff Anderson stood in the door when Jackson rode up. A middle-aged man with a large belly, he had a handlebar mustache and dark hair frosted with gray. His black, squinty eyes stared straight through Jackson.

"Come on in, son." He held the door open for

Jackson to walk past.

Jackson set the saddlebags on the sheriff's desk. "Miss Wagner is not in Wylder. Sheriff Wylder is out looking for her."

Sheriff Anderson nodded his head. "It's you I'm interested in."

Jackson pulled a chair up to the sheriff's desk. "I heard you had a couple of questions to ask me."

Sheriff Anderson sat on the corner of his desk and folded his arms. "What do you know about Rex Conway's death?"

Jackson shrugged. "Nothing. I was in my bed asleep when it happened."

Sheriff Anderson shook his head. "I have a witness who says he rode up right after you shot Mr. Conway. He found you standing over the body with a gun in your hand."

Jackson stared. "I was in Wylder asleep. I found out about the murder the next morning."

Sheriff Anderson smiled a mirthless grin. "Do you have anyone who can verify your story?"

"I'm single, sheriff. I sleep alone."

Sheriff Anderson pulled out a set of handcuffs and snapped them around his wrists. Jackson stared at them. "What is this?"

"I am charging you with Rex Conway's murder."

Jackson rose to his feet. "You can't do that. I was in Wylder."

"Without a witness, Mr. Daniels, you can't prove it wasn't you."

Jackson struggled with the handcuffs.

"This is my town. I am the law, and I do what I please." He made a motion with his hand. Three men walked into the sheriff's office. William Smythe walked through the door first, grinning from ear to ear. The other two were men Jackson had not seen before.

"Allow me to introduce my friends," William said. "James Redding and Porter Richards."

Jackson had their measure in a matter of minutes. James looked to be a little under six foot and pure evil. He had black hair and brown soulless eyes. Jackson noted the knife in his boot and the calluses on the palm of his hand and up his pointer finger. He liked knives and knew how to use them. His sneer told Jackson he had no respect for anyone.

Porter Richards was a little taller than James, muscular, and built like a bull. He had red hair and eyes as black as midnight. His hands were the size of hams. He clenched and unclenched them as he stared at Jackson as if anxious to get down to business. He seemed accustomed to using his fists to get what he wanted.

The three men blocked the door, surrounding Jackson on three sides.

Jackson studied the sheriff.

Sheriff Anderson couldn't meet his eyes. He patted his well-padded shirt pocket and walked a wide berth around Jackson to tug the shades down over the windows. He turned back to the three men. "Let's get to it. I don't want anyone to walk in."

Jackson narrowed his gaze. "These boys paid you to lure me here so they can beat on me, kill me, or both?"

Sheriff Anderson rose to his feet. "There will be no killing." He grinned. "At least not until you're hanged for shooting Rex Conway in the back."

Jackson knew arguing would do no good. "In order to hang me, a federal judge will have to pronounce me guilty in court."

Sheriff Anderson chuckled, "Not around here, son."

Jackson shrugged. "Are you forgetting Sheriff Wylder? He knows I came to Lonetree. He sent me with the saddlebags. If I don't return, he's going to come asking questions. He won't quit until he finds out what happened to me." He tilted his chair. "They don't call him Hound Dog Wylder for nothing." Jackson had no idea if they did or didn't. He lied to save his skin. He knew without a doubt Sheriff Anderson would hang him on William Smythe's say so. Jackson's words to Maryanne flashed through his mind. *"Nothing is so bad you can't tell the truth."* Jackson winced. He should have let her explain.

Sheriff Anderson held his hand up to William and his friends. "Daniels has a point." He frowned. "I'll send a telegram to the judge tomorrow. In the meantime, you boys can help Mr. Daniels to his cell, but no rough stuff. I don't want any marks on him for the judge to see." He patted the pocket of his shirt. "I'm going to walk outside now and have a smoke. I can't be in the room when you welcome Mr. Daniels to Lonetree."

Jackson rolled his shoulders. "You going to leave me cuffed?" he asked. "It's three to one." He glanced at William. "Are you city boys too scared to face me like men?"

Sheriff Anderson stopped.

William sneered. "I'm not scared of you. I've been waiting to mess up your face since I found out

Maryanne stayed at the livery in Wylder."

Jackson yawned. "You're so worried you won't win you had the sheriff hobble me and brought two friends to help you out?"

Sheriff Anderson stepped in front of Jackson as Porter roared, and James pulled the knife from his boot. "No! I said no visible marks." He turned to Jackson and removed his handcuffs. "Never let it be said I am not a fair man."

Jackson paid no attention. He jumped to his feet and punched William in the face. He knocked Porter on his backside and kicked the blade from James's hand.

Sheriff Anderson swallowed and backed hurriedly toward the door. "I'll go have my cigar now."

The door shut behind him, and the lock turned. Jackson shook his hands to get the blood flowing and danced in place. Porter jumped to his feet and advanced with a shout of anger. William shook his head and rushed at Jackson. Jackson rolled his shoulders and tucked his chin. He'd been in fights with bullies before.

Twenty minutes later, Jackson wiped the blood from his face and looked around the sheriff's office. The last thing intact was the sheriff's oak desk. James lay unconscious over the remnants of a broken chair. Porter lay face down beside the potbelly stove, making a puddle of blood with the gash on his head.

William was the last one on his feet. His eye was swollen shut, and his lip resembled a turtle. "I will see you hanged for touching my property."

It took Jackson a second or two to realize William referred to Maryanne. His gaze fell on William's right hand. He had on a signet ring with a snake in the center. "Snake ring" were the last two words the little immigrant girl said the night Jackson found her beaten nigh to death in Wylder. He hadn't read Maryanne's letter. It remained tucked inside his shirt pocket. Jackson figured he knew what it said. He now understood everything Maryanne did, why she robbed the bank and ran away, why she lied about her name and why she went pale whenever William's name came up. He also knew why she didn't turn herself in. Sheriff Anderson would hand her back to William on a silver plate.

The room whirled around Jackson's head. Any minute and he would pass out. Jackson would be in a cell, unable to help Maryanne. William would be free to hunt her down and make her comply with her father's wishes. There was one thing he could do to make sure William never touched Maryanne again. "She's not your property anymore. She's married to me." Jackson shrugged his conscience off. Maryanne asked if he would marry her if things were different. He never answered, but yes, he would marry her. He just didn't tell her quick enough.

William glared at him with pure rage. He took a step toward Jackson and fell face-first to the floor, out cold.

Jackson fell to his knees. Sheriff Anderson walked back into the room as blackness claimed him.

Chapter Eleven

"I want to see the man who shot my baby in the back."

Jackson looked up from his seat on the narrow cot in his cell. Just what he needed, visitors. He had eight stitches above one eye and five across one cheek. Sheriff Anderson told the doctor he resisted arrest. The report was correct, and he resisted his arrest to this very minute.

An older lady dressed in lavender silk strolled into the room on the arm of the sheriff. She held a lace kerchief to her nose and tip-toed across the floor as if afraid the wooden planks would give her a disease. Jackson rose to his feet. He wasn't a killer, and his granny trained him to be a gentleman despite the circumstances.

Mrs. Conway stopped short and gasped. "You! Are you the one who shot my Rex in the back?" Her hand fluttered over her heart as if afraid it would overheat any second.

"No, ma'am, I did not," Jackson answered. He stared the woman in the eyes as he said the words, so she understood.

She gasped and took a step back. "You deny it? First, you shoot my son, and then you lie to cover it up." Her expression hardened. "I hope you hang." She took a step forward. "I shall sit in the front row and watch you die. My baby deserved more in this life, and you took it away from him. I want to know why. What did my Rexy do to you?"

Jackson studied her face. "Nothing. We never crossed paths." He was an intelligent man. What Maryanne didn't say in her letter, Jackson pieced together. "How well did you know your son, Mrs. Conway?"

Sheriff Anderson made a noise and tried to usher Mrs. Conway from the room. "It's best if we go. Nothing can be gained from listening to this murderer."

Mrs. Conway dug in. "I want to hear what he has to say. I want to look into his cold dead eyes and hear why." She shook the sheriff's hand off and walked closer to the bars. "Tell me what my baby did to deserve to die so young."

Jackson had plenty of reasons why Rex Conway deserved to die. He didn't want the sheriff or Mrs. Conway to know he knew their dirty secret. "Why not ask William Smythe? He was there when your son died. I was in Wylder in my own bed, asleep."

Mrs. Conway narrowed her eyes. "Are you suggesting poor William knows something about my Rex? He said he found you standing over my baby." She stepped closer. "I believe him. Why would William lie about Rex's death?"

Jackson shrugged. "You should ask yourself the same question. How many times have they lied for each other, Mrs. Conway?"

Mrs. Conway lifted her nose into the air. "I already gave William the reward money for Rex's killer."

"Then you wasted it because I'm not the killer."

Mrs. Conway couldn't resist the urge to tell more.

"Poor William needed the money. Bernard Smythe cut him off without a dime until William married some peasant girl the family knows and produced an heir. I'm told the girl is missing." She chuckled. "It serves Bernard right. He should have married William to my daughter Elizabeth. They are so much better suited."

Sheriff Anderson took her by the arm and insisted he escort her from the room. Mrs. Conway allowed herself to be led away while she rambled on and on about her daughter's beauty.

Jackson sat back down. No wonder William lost his temper when Jackson mentioned Maryanne married him. Now, he would not get his money. Jackson smiled a mirthless smile. He lied to help Maryanne. Wherever she went, she deserved better. He took her letter from his pocket and sniffed. Her scent filled his nostrils. Longing filled his heart. If she were here, he'd tell her he understood and apologize for hurting her. He hoped he had the chance to ask for Maryanne's forgiveness. Jackson unfolded her letter and read it for the hundredth time. Her pleading tugged at his heartstrings. She did what she had to do to survive. Maryanne was right. Some men did deserve to be shot in the back, and Jackson couldn't fault her for it.

Sheriff Wylder paid him a visit two days after his arrest. He was unable to locate Maryanne. Jackson ignored the tightening in his stomach. Where would she go? Her tear-stained face haunted him every time he closed his eyes.

Sheriff Wylder took exception to Jackson being in jail. After a very heated conversation with Sheriff Anderson, he stopped by Jackson's cell. "They're railroading you, Jackson. I don't know why William

Smythe swears you killed Rex Conway when I know you didn't." He shook his head. "I don't know what I can do to help, but I'll think of something."

Jackson motioned for him to come closer. In quick whispered words, he explained everything.

Sheriff Wylder digested the information for several minutes. Then, he nodded his head. "We need to find Maryanne and the whore. Her testimony is all we have."

"I agree," Jackson said.

The judge would arrive in two weeks. They didn't have a lot of time. "I'll put out the word amongst the girls," Sheriff Wylder said. "I know they keep in touch. One of them can get word to Sadie."

A shiny black carriage rolled up to the sheriff's office and stopped outside the door. An older gentleman stepped out in a gray traveling coat with silver buttons and a black top hat.

"Who is he?" Jackson asked.

"Mr. Wagner, president of Wagner Trust," Sheriff Wylder answered.

Jackson had a perfect view of the sheriff's office from his cell.

Mr. Wagner stepped inside and stopped. He leaned on his marble-handled cane while he waited to be noticed.

He was in his late fifties, of medium height and build, with graying hair and cold brown eyes. Another gentleman stepped from the carriage and joined Mr. Wagner. He was at least a decade older, with white hair and ice blue eyes. Taller than Mr. Wagner and portly, he carried an air of importance and rapped his cane on the sheriff's desk to get their attention.

"We have come for the girl," the older gentleman announced. He introduced himself as Bernard Smythe, President of Smythe Bank and Trust in New York City.

Sheriff Anderson shook his hand.

Sheriff Wylder didn't appear impressed. Neither was Jackson. Maryanne had been in Wylder for a month, and her father hadn't noticed her absence or didn't care. He didn't know Jackson hadn't brought her back to Lonetree, and Jackson had been in jail for two days.

"She is not here," Branch answered. "We don't know where she went, but we're looking for her."

Mr. Smythe's bushy eyebrows tilted to a frown. "This is what comes from pampering her, Phineas. William will have his work cut out for him to break her spirit. I told you we should have married them the instant we signed the contract."

Phineas Wagner shrugged. "Maryanne wanted to wait until fall. This is the last time I listen to her pleading. I shall have her whipped as soon as we get her home."

Jackson's head snapped up.

Mr. Smythe glared. "William will see to it. If we did this my way, Maryanne would be about to deliver my grandchild." He rolled his eyes. "It is irritating how much you coddle her, Phineas."

Sheriff Anderson gazed from one to the other. "I imagine you want to count the stolen money, too?"

He indicated the saddlebags sitting on his desk.

Mr. Wagner stepped to the door and motioned for his driver to come inside. "We shall count it after dinner. I will be at home. You can reach us there as soon as you have news on Maryanne."

His servant took the saddlebags, and the three men left.

Jackson stared after them. He couldn't believe what he just heard. Break her spirit? Whip her? Fury coursed through him. He remembered the way she looked when he first laid eyes on her, bloody and wounded on his stall floor. Maryanne weighed next to nothing. These men were all larger than she was. He remembered how she cringed and jerked away from him the first couple of weeks. Jackson blamed William as much as her father. After reading Maryanne's letter, he wished he had another chance to whip the bastard.

He patted her folded note in his pocket. "We will win, Maryanne, because we are survivors. And once this is finished, I will find you and bring you home."

The days were long and endless. William and his cohorts liked to visit and bait Jackson. He ignored them. When they got too aggressive, Jackson got up and walked toward the bars. The bullies would leave. None of them wanted to be within arm's reach.

Jackson wondered where Maryanne went and if she found someone to take her in. His gut twisted every time he thought about her. He never knew a woman could have such strength. In her letter, she mentioned growing up as an only child with no mother and a father who expected his servants to raise her. Mr. Wagner had not the patience nor the inclination to be a parent. According to her letter, the Smythe's were the closest thing Maryanne had to family. And after what Jackson learned about them, he wondered how Maryanne survived as long as she had.

Jackson paced his cell and considered possible places Maryanne could have gone. She said in her letter she went to the one place he would never look. He had no idea where such a place might be.

The days passed one at a time with nerve-grating repetition. Branch Wylder visited two more times, but he came empty-handed. No one knew where Sadie or Maryanne was.

Chief Justice Joseph Fisher arrived in Lonetree on a Friday. He was in his seventies with a full head of white hair. He visited the jail on his way to the hotel and spoke with Sheriff Anderson before making his way back to Jackson.

He shook Jackson's hand through the bars. "It's nice to meet you, son. I'm here to see justice is done. If you're innocent, I'll order your release. If not, I'll order your death just as quick."

Jackson nodded. He'd heard about Judge Fisher. He was as good a judge as could be found in Wyoming Territory. Jackson frowned as the judge walked away. He wasn't sure if he should be worried or relieved his day of reckoning had arrived.

Chapter Twelve

Jackson sat before the judge in the town hall. Today, it doubled as a courtroom. Sheriff Wylder sat beside him on a stiff-backed wooden chair. Sheriff Anderson and William Smythe sat to their right. The courtroom filled with friends. Most of the people in Wylder sat behind him. The Conway's and William's two friends, Porter and James, sat behind Sheriff Anderson.

The judge called the court to order and asked for the charges against Jackson. Sheriff Anderson read the charge of murder and called his first witness. William Smythe rose to his feet and swore to tell the truth.

"I went riding for exercise, enjoying the evening air when I heard a man shout. I suspected trouble and went to offer my assistance. I heard a gunshot and spurred my horse forward." He pointed at Jackson. "I found this man standing over the body of my friend Rex Conway. Jackson Daniels had a smoking gun in his hand. He shot my friend in cold blood. I demand justice be done."

Judge Fisher turned to Jackson. "Who represents you?"

"I defend myself," Jackson answered. He approached William. "Where did you find Rex Conway's body?"

William stared. "You know."

"Answer the question," Judge Fisher ordered.

William glared at Jackson.

" Five miles south of Lonetree," Sheriff Anderson cut in.

Jackson nodded. "Do you often take your horse on an evening ride so far out of town? To be specific, on a Friday night?"

William shrugged. "I don't know. I guess."

Jackson paced in front of him. "Isn't there a cabin a couple of miles farther south? The way I understand it, you and your friends like to take whores out there on Friday and Saturday nights."

William leaned back in his chair. "No. I know nothing about a cabin anywhere near here."

Jackson stopped in front of William. "Will you show us what position I was in when you saw me with a gun standing over the victim?"

William stood up. "What difference does it make? You shot him. Are you trying to torture his poor mother with the details of your crime?"

Jackson glanced at Judge Fisher. "I am trying to verify the details as the witness stated them."

Judge Fisher nodded. "Show us what you saw."

William looked around for help. Everyone stared. With an exclamation, he pointed his finger as if it were a gun and aimed down at an imaginary object on the ground.

Mrs. Conway began to cry.

Jackson ignored her and asked for the undertaker so he could question him. He asked the man to explain the difference between a close-range and long-range bullet wound. The undertaker explained gunshot wounds acquired within a few feet contain one round central wound. Gunshots acquired long distance have a smaller central wound accompanied by several surrounding pellet holes. The undertaker gave his professional statement about the wound. The murderer shot Rex Conway in the back from a distance.

William Smythe growled and hit the table in front of him with his fist.

Miss Gwen, the town madame, entered the town hall with several of her girls. Miss Gwen was in her early thirties and the wealthiest woman in town. She packed a lot of influence and power. Nobody talked about it, but everybody knew it. They took seats in the back while the undertaker gave his testimony. Their appearance caused quite a stir. The married women of Lonetree got up and left with their noses in the air, dragging their husbands with them.

Miss Gwen motioned for her girls to stay where they were and walked to the front of the building. She informed the judge her girls had something to say.

William Smythe rose to his feet. Anger shot from his dark eyes. "Surely you aren't going to allow the whores to speak?"

Judge Fisher stared. "Why not?"

William scoffed. "Because they're women, and they're whores."

Judge Fisher leaned over his desk. "Sit down, or I will have you arrested for disrupting my court."

William stared. The judge stared back. William sat.

One by one, Miss Gwen's girls testified about William Smythe and Rex Conway. They told in detail the horrible things they suffered at their hands. When Jackson asked them where the situations occurred, they told the judge about William's cabin eight miles south of town.

The building buzzed with discussion.

Judge Fisher pounded his gavel to get everyone's attention. He glared at William. "You lied about your reason for being outside of town. You lied about seeing Jackson Daniels standing over the body of Rex Conway. The only true statement in your entire testimony is Rex Conway's death. What are you not telling us about that night?"

"He's not telling you about me," a voice said from the back of the courtroom. A woman fitting Sadie's description appeared in the doorway, followed by Maryanne.

Jackson's heart leaped into his throat. He stared at her, unable to believe his eyes.

"Who are you?" Judge Fisher demanded.

"My name is Sadie White. I was with Rex Conway the night he got shot."

Mrs. Conway rose to her feet. Her eyes narrowed. "My boy never mentioned you."

"Come in, Miss White, and tell us what you know," the judge invited, waving his hand in her direction. "Sit down, Mrs. Conway, unless you want to be escorted outside."

She sat.

Jackson rose to his feet. He drank in the sight of Maryanne's beautiful face. She wore her pink gingham dress. The one she wore when she tried to make him soup. The room whirled. His gaze roamed over her as she approached. When she lifted her head, he recognized the look in her eyes and knew what she planned to do. She came to confess to Rex's murder. "No," he said. "No, Maryanne. I won't let you." He looked up at the judge. "I don't want them to give their testimony."

Judge Fisher swore. "You too? I will listen to what they have to say. Either sit down, Mr. Daniels, or I will have you removed from the court as well."

Jackson sat back down. His mind whirled. How the hell could he get her out of this? He stared at Maryanne, willing her to look at him. She kept her gaze on the judge, refusing to meet Jackson's eyes. She walked with Sadie to the front of the room and stopped.

Jackson turned his gaze to Sadie. One eyebrow rose in surprise at her appearance. She wore a blue calico dress with her blonde hair pinned in curls atop her head. Her dress portrayed both taste and fashion, with slim lines in the front and an elegant bustle in the back. She looked like a lady. One would never guess her former occupation .

"Start at the beginning," Judge Fisher ordered.

"My name is Sadie White. I used to work for Miss Gwen." She blushed. "You know, above the saloon."

Judge Fisher motioned her forward. "And you?" He pointed at Maryanne.

"Maryanne Wagner," she replied.

"What do you have to tell us we don't already know?" Judge Fisher looked back at Sadie.

Sadie glanced at William. Porter and James leaned forward in their chairs. She took a couple of steps closer to Jackson and Branch Wylder. "I can tell you who shot Rex Conway and why."

Everyone spoke at once. The onlookers buzzed with excitement.

"He did it!" Mrs. Conway screamed, pointing her finger at Jackson.

William, Porter, and James glanced at each other. James slipped the knife from his boot. Sheriff Anderson jumped to his feet and objected to Sadie giving her testimony. He had the killer and wanted Jackson to hang.

Judge Fisher pounded his gavel to get everyone to quiet down.

"If anyone in this court speaks again without permission, I will have you all removed." He gazed out over the audience. Then he smiled at Sadie. "Go ahead, Miss White, and tell us what happened."

"Miss Gwen said I had a customer. When I saw Rex Conway, I told him I was sick and couldn't take anybody else. He tricked me into coming downstairs with him. I told him I didn't want to go with him. I knew what he did to the other girls out at their cabin." Sadie took a breath.

"My Rex wouldn't be caught dead in a saloon with a woman like her," Mrs. Conway bellowed.

Judge Fisher pounded his gavel. He motioned for Sheriff Anderson to remove Mrs. Conway from the court.

Sadie told them about waking up on Rex's horse and Rex beating her.

Sheriff Anderson returned and stood against the east wall where he could see everything.

"Then I heard a shot. Mr. Rex grabbed his chest and fell in the dirt." Her voice shook as she recounted what happened. She glanced at Maryanne.

"Well?" the judge said.

"I shot him," Maryanne said. She gazed up at the judge without flinching.

Jackson groaned. His heart thudded and lodged in

his throat, choking him. He wanted to grab her and run. Somehow, he had to get her the hell out of here.

"Well, well, well," William muttered. His gaze focused on Maryanne.

"She saved my life," Sadie added. "If Miss Maryanne hadn't come, I would've died."

A murmur went through the crowd.

Jackson glanced at William. His face turned red with anger. William exchanged glances with Porter and James.

"Go on," the judge said.

"We heard another horse coming down the road behind us. We figured William Smythe and his friends, Porter Richards and James Redding, were heading out to the cabin. We knew they would kill us if they saw us. Miss Maryanne got worried for me. She knew William and his friends would come looking for me once they found Rex. She gave me one hundred dollars to go far away where they couldn't find me. I went away like she said and got a real job. I owe Miss Maryanne everything."

The courtroom went crazy. Jackson kept his eye on William and his cohorts.

They glanced at each other, and William nodded.

Jackson's chest tightened. If the judge didn't hang her, William and his friends would kill her. Jackson looked over at Maryanne's father. Mr. Wagner did not appear to be concerned. He sat stiffly beside Mr. Smythe. Both men could have been carved from stone. So much for any help from them.

"You have her confession," William said. "Hang the bitch."

Everyone gasped. Judge Fisher looked from one to

the other. He leaned around to gaze at Jackson. "You're free to go, Mr. Daniels." He nodded at Sheriff Anderson. "Unlock his cuffs and give him back his guns."

Sheriff Anderson frowned as he walked over and unlocked Jackson's cuffs. "Are you sure this is what you want, Judge? I've seen Mr. Daniels fight. He's a violent man."

The judge turned to the sheriff and glared.

Sheriff Anderson backed up. "All right, I'm doing it." He sent a deputy to the sheriff's office to retrieve the revolvers.

Branch Wylder smiled and slapped Jackson on the shoulder.

Jackson nodded at the judge to let him know he heard, but he didn't move. His heart remained in his throat. Why did Maryanne put herself in danger? Why did she confess to Rex's murder? Wherever she went, she'd been safe. No one knew her location, and no one knew what she'd done besides Sadie. Until Maryanne wrote her letter to him, that is, and then he knew.

Maryanne never turned her head once to look at anyone but the judge. Her father said nothing. He stared straight ahead and ignored her. Jackson's gaze returned to Maryanne. Her father hadn't laid eyes on her for weeks, and he didn't even glance her way. What kind of man cared nothing for his child?

Jackson's heart ached for her. He could not imagine a life without the love and support of his father.

"Miss Wagner, you are free to go, as well," Judge Fisher said. "Rex Conway received justice for his crimes. No charges will be brought against you." He hit his gavel on the table.

William rose to his feet. "I object. Miss Wagner should hang. She admitted murdering Rex in cold blood."

The judge glared at him. "Miss Wagner is free to go."

William interrupted, "I admit we visit the saloon and the girls when we're in Lonetree, but you can't prove we did anything more than ride them." He sneered at Sadie. "To accept the word of a whore is ridiculous." He glared at the judge. "It's unethical. My father will see you stripped of your position."

"I agree," Mrs. Conway chimed in, edging her way back into the town hall. "I demand you hang the girl for the death of my son."

"How many girls died at the cabin?" Judge Fisher asked Miss Gwen, ignoring William and Mrs. Conway. He motioned for Sheriff Anderson to take Mrs. Conway out again.

"Two of mine," Miss Gwen answered.

Sheriff Wylder raised his hand. "If you'll give me a moment. I want to tell the court about a murder in Wylder." He recounted the events in Wylder when the Irish girl died. "The last thing the girl said was the man who attacked her wore a snake ring."

Every eye went to William's right hand. He twisted his snake ring back and forth with his finger. William glared at Sheriff Wylder then turned to his friends with a nod. They nodded back.

A deputy appeared at Jackson's side and handed Jackson his guns. He strapped them on and took his seat. He couldn't take his eyes from Maryanne. It was courageous and stupid for her to confess to Rex's killing. She did it for him. He knew it, and it angered him. She shouldn't have put herself at risk. He knew the danger she faced from William and his friends.

Judge Fisher thanked Miss Gwen, the girls, and Sadie for having the courage to stand up and tell their side of things. Then he dismissed them. Maryanne and Sadie turned around. Jackson wanted to catch Maryanne's hand when she drew abreast of him, but he didn't.

James slipped one of the knives from his boots and handed it to William. Jackson frowned. Something wasn't right. William's gaze remained focused on Judge Fisher. His friends were poised for action. Their anger and excitement were obvious from his seat across the room.

Sheriff Wylder nudged him. "Be ready. They have something planned."

Jackson nodded and waited to see what happened.

Judge Fisher leaned forward. "William Smythe, Porter Richards, and James Redding. You are under arrest for the deaths of Emily Rose, Mary Turner, and the Irish girl in Wylder."

Sheriff Anderson stared at the judge. "What?" He just stepped back into the room in time to hear the judge put the three men under arrest.

William, Porter, and James jumped to their feet. Branch pulled his gun and cocked it. All three men froze.

Bernard Smythe came to life in an instant. He rose from his seat beside Mr. Wagner and barreled toward the judge. "Now see here! You can't arrest William. I paid good money for his protection." He turned to Sheriff Anderson. "Do the job I paid you for and tell this judge my boy is innocent."

Judge Fisher smiled. "It's like that, is it?" He turned to the deputy standing nearby. "Lock Sheriff Anderson and the rest of these men up. The sheriff will stand trial for negligence of duty and accepting bribes. The other three will hang for murder."

Bernard Smythe started forward.

Judge Fisher glared. "Stay where you are or I'll charge you with contempt."

Bernard Smythe stopped in his tracks.

The deputy cuffed Sheriff Anderson and led him away.

Jackson turned around. He couldn't see Maryanne anywhere. She must have gone outside with the rest of the women. Jackson approved of her decision to leave. William and his friends would not go down without a fight. He faced the front in time to see William leap from his seat and jump across the table. He had Judge Fisher in front of him with James's knife to his neck before anyone realized what happened.

"Stay back," he commanded Sheriff Wylder. "I'll kill the judge if you come any closer."

Branch narrowed his gaze. He glanced at Jackson, and Jackson nodded.

Jackson pulled his gun and pointed it at William Smythe. Sheriff Wylder kept his gun pointed at Porter and James. Jackson stood still beside his chair, waiting for an opportunity.

William took the old man with him, backing out of the town hall with slow steps. The townspeople scattered. William was unfamiliar with the building, and when he turned to look behind him, Jackson shot. The bullet hit William in the back. He fell to the floor with a thud.

Jackson froze when he realized what he did. This is what Maryanne felt when she shot Rex. He had no guilt, no cowardice, and no shame. He shot a man in the back to save a life. The realization stunned him. The act was not as black and white as he supposed.

Judge Fisher fell to the floor with William. James slipped the knife from his other boot and turned toward Branch. Sheriff Wylder shot him between the eyes. Porter pulled his gun and ran for the door. He aimed it at one of the deputies and squeezed off a shot. Sheriff Wylder turned and shot him, too. The judge rose to his feet and dusted himself off. Everyone froze.

"Are you all right, Your Honor?" Branch asked.

"I'm fine. It takes more than they have to put me down." He glanced around the room. "Are they all dead?"

Sheriff Wylder checked. "Yes."

"Call the undertaker. Court is dismissed. You can all go." He righted his robe and walked back to the table. With a stern face, he pounded his gavel.

The townspeople filtered back inside the town hall, wanting to know what happened. The noise level grew making it difficult to hear.

Judge Fisher motioned for Branch Wylder to come closer. They held a quiet conversation. When Mrs. Conway descended on them, Bernard Smythe stood by her side.

"You let them shoot my boy," Bernard Smythe said. He glowered at Judge Fisher.

"Perhaps you do not understand our position, Judge Fisher," Mrs. Conway continued. "We demand you put a bounty on Maryanne Wagner's head. She shot my baby in cold blood. She deserves to hang."

"I want Jackson Daniels hanged for murdering my son," Bernard added. "The nonsense the whores were spouting is ridiculous. I agree with William. They shouldn't be allowed in court. No woman has the right to testify, period. Their word means nothing."

Mrs. Conway glanced at Bernard and harrumphed.

The judge looked over the rims of his glasses. "The way I see it, Rex Conway and William Smythe received justice for their crimes. I don't know how many more times I need to say court dismissed. Jackson Daniels and Maryanne Wagner are free, and they will remain free." His eyes snapped blue fire.

Mrs. Conway turned red. She opened her mouth to dispute the judge, but he stopped her. "If I hear any more from either of you, I'll send telegrams to several editor friends I have on the east coast. I'll relate in detail Rex's and William's interludes with ladies of questionable morals here in Lonetree as well as Wylder. I'll also discuss how those three women died. Your sons had some…unusual habits, and I shall ensure the story makes the front page of every newspaper. Think how your friends will react once they hear the sordid details of your sons' last few days."

Mrs. Conway read the warning on the judge's face. She snapped her mouth shut and sailed from the room with her head high in the air. Bernard Smythe narrowed his gaze. He slid his hands into his pockets and glared.

"If you think you have more influence and power than I, think again. I don't play nice, Mr. Smythe. I play to win." Judge Fisher stared him down.

Bernard Smythe gave the judge one more glare and walked away.

The judge swore in one of the deputies as a temporary sheriff until a new one could be elected. He deputized two more men in the meantime.

Jackson shook Judge Fisher's hand. "Thank you, sir."

"Don't thank me. If I were you, I'd find Miss Wagner and thank her. It took a lot of courage to turn herself in." He stopped. "I would also thank Miss Gwen. Without her girls, none of the four men's secrets would have been told."

Jackson knew it. "I plan to, sir." They shook hands, and Jackson walked outside. He searched the crowds milling about retelling the events of the trial. He couldn't find Maryanne or Sadie.

Jackson growled with anger. Where the hell would she go? Why would she leave when he had so much to say to her? Would she go back to Wylder? He knew Lonetree held no appeal for her. She may have gone back to the livery to wait for him.

Jackson got on his horse and rode back to Wylder with Branch. They arrived about midnight. Jackson rubbed his horse down and put him away in his stall. He paused when he walked past Maryanne's door, amused he thought of it as such. She had been gone for nigh on a month. His chest tightened. He knocked , hoping to see her sweet face like he used to. No one answered. Jackson opened the door to an empty room. She hadn't returned to Wylder or him.

Jackson leaned his head against the door frame. Where would she go? Why not come to him? There was no reason for her to hide with William dead. He knew the answer as soon as he asked the question. Jackson told her to go. This was on him.

Chapter Thirteen

Maryanne swung her braid over her shoulder and grabbed the horse's hoof. She held it with one hand and aligned the horseshoe with the curve of the hoof. She took down the tin of nails from her workbench and pounded one in with her hammer. She grabbed another nail and pounded it in, too.

"Miss Maryanne, you have another customer. His horse slipped on the ice, and he wants you to put shoe studs on."

"Okay, give me a minute, John." She pounded the remaining nails into the mare's hoof and let go of her leg. Maryanne straightened. Shoeing horses made her back ache. She stretched and rolled her shoulders before untying the mare and leading her back to the owner. She patted the horse as she walked past. "Where is the customer?" She had two more horses to do before she finished for the day.

"Up front," John called.

Maryanne walked through the blacksmith shop. She rounded the corner and came face to face with the last person she expected to see, Jackson.

A million scenarios ran through her mind since she left Lonetree six months ago. This one never made its debut. Maryanne wore a heavy leather apron over her dress to protect it. Part of her hair escaped her tight braid and hung in her face. She tucked her hands behind her back, out of sight. They were dirty, and her fingernails were broken.

She swallowed. "What are you doing here?" She didn't think she would ever see him again.

Jackson's gaze started at the top of her head and worked its way down to her feet.

Maryanne fidgeted with the seam inside her pocket. The minute stretched into an awkward silence. "What do you want?" she asked, shifting from one foot to the other. She looked worse than a mess, and she knew it.

Jackson's gaze rose to hers. "I want shoe studs put on my horse. He slipped. I came to the closest farrier." Jackson frowned. "Where is the workman?"

Maryanne swallowed. It would be best to keep it all business. He hadn't come for her, so the least she could do is treat him like anybody else. She could examine her heart later to check for new cracks. "I do the horseshoes. Let's see what you got."

Jackson hesitated for several seconds as if digesting the situation. "You shoe horses?"

"Yes," Maryanne answered. "Where's your horse?" *Jackson is a normal man needing help with a horseshoe. Nothing to get excited about,* she said to her heart. Her heart rate increased despite the lies. Her hands trembled, and her knees shook. *Get a hold of yourself. It's just Jackson.* She ignored the scent of his cedarwood soap and the leather smell she associated with him. Maryanne kept her gaze forward. She couldn't look at his handsome face or drown in his beautiful eyes. If she ignored him, she could be this close to him and not want to hold onto him.

"Have you been in Boston this whole time?"

Jackson asked. He looked irritated.

Maryanne stilled. "It was the one place I thought you would never look."

Jackson stared. He shook his head in amazement. "You're right. The reason I'm here now is Granny died."

"So you weren't looking for me?" Maryanne cringed as soon as she asked the question. Of course, he wasn't. He never wanted to see her again. Curse her big mouth.

"I have been. I mean, I am." He removed his top hat and ran a hand through his hair. "I've been everywhere searching for you. I went all over Wyoming Territory, to Omaha, to Houston." He shook his head. "I even went to Salt Lake City." He undid his tie and shoved his hands in his trouser pockets.

She realized with a start he wore formal clothes and, boy, did he look good. His tailored suit with a wingtip collar fit his broad shoulders like a glove. His narrow waist and lean hips were accentuated by the cut of his trousers. He had on a snowy white shirt and a black tie.

"Are you on your way to a party?" A pang of envy shot through her. It had been six months. His life could be very different by now. "Are you married?" she blurted out. They stopped outside by his horse. Darn her big mouth.

Jackson looked surprised. "No, on both counts." His gaze sharpened. "Are you?"

Maryanne shook her head.

A slow smile spread over his face. "Good." He untied his horse from the hitching post and led him into the back. "He doesn't hold still very well." He glanced down at his formal clothes in frustration. "I won't be able to help you." He glanced around. "Is there a man around who can help?" He tied his horse to the rail inside her work area.

Maryanne couldn't decide if she should be offended that he doubted her ability or flattered he wanted to help.

"I can handle him," she answered. She took her twitch and slipped it over his horse's top lip. She tightened the chain and handed Jackson the handle. His horse stilled. Not a muscle moved.

Maryanne moved behind the horse and lifted his rear leg. "You've had studs before," she commented. "It will be faster since I don't have to punch holes." She took out a stud plug and cleaned out the hole.

Jackson stood beside her, watching. Maryanne got her tin of studs and screwed one in. She did the same to the next one.

"How do you know how to do this?" he asked. "Why are you in Boston? Why are you working at a farrier? And while we are on the subject, why did you leave after the trial without saying a word? Why did you come to Lonetree in the first place?" He ran his hand through his hair a second time. Once the questions started, they came one after the other. "You could have been hanged for murder."

Maryanne reached for another plug. "I know."

Jackson's gaze bored into her. "How did you know about the trial?"

Maryanne dipped her head. "It was all over the newspapers. The Conway's, Richards, Redding's, and Smythe's are big news." She grimaced. "Everything they do makes the front page."

Jackson nodded. "You didn't answer my question. Why did you come to Lonetree?"

Maryanne lifted her gaze to his. "I told you I would fix it. I made the mess, not you. You shouldn't be arrested and hanged for something I did." She dipped her head to screw in a post. "I would never be able to live with myself if you died because of me." She kept her head down so he couldn't see her tears. Going to Lonetree frightened the life out of her.

"Why did you leave again?" he asked. "William Smythe is dead. There is no threat. You're free."

She set the hoof on the ground and walked around to the other leg. She paused by the horse's side. "You never wanted to see me again," she whispered. Her heart rose to her throat. It hurt to think about. It hurt even worse to see him with his hands cuffed together in Lonetree.

Jackson stepped close to her and stroked her cheek. "I got angry. I found your saddlebags, and I was back in Boston again, accused of something I didn't do. I thought things were black and white, one way or the other, with no in-between, but I was wrong."

Maryanne squeezed her eyes to keep the tears from leaking out. It didn't work.

Jackson leaned over and wiped them away with the pad of his thumb. "I found myself doing the things I had such contempt for." He lifted her chin so he could gaze into her eyes. "I lied to Smythe to keep him from searching for you." A wry smile touched his full lips. "I also shot him in the back."

Maryanne gaped at him. "You shot William in the back?"

Jackson nodded. "If you'd stuck around, you

would've known." He described the situation. "When William moved, I had a chance to rescue the judge, and I took it." He shrugged. "I want to apologize for not letting you explain. I should have let you tell your side of the story."

Maryanne sighed. "It's not important," she said and picked up the last hoof.

"It *is* important," Jackson argued. "If I had listened, we would have figured out a way to make it better."

Maryanne's heart did double-time. We? She frowned. "What lie did you tell William about me?" she asked. Curiosity ran strong in her blood.

Jackson cleared his throat. "I told him we were married."

"What?" Maryanne screwed the post in and looked up at Jackson.

He shrugged. "He would have come for you. I had to think of something to stop him."

"Oh." Hope wilted to a pile of ashes on the ground. Maryanne took another post and screwed it in.

"I hoped you wanted to make it real," Jackson said. "You did ask me if I would marry you one night outside your door."

Maryanne pitched forward and almost fell. He remembered? Jackson caught her around the waist.

She straightened. "Can you repeat the last part?"

His hazel eyes stared into her soul. "I missed you, Maryanne. There hasn't been a day I haven't thought about you and wondered if you were warm and safe. I've searched everywhere I could think of for you and came up empty-handed. You've driven me crazy wondering where you were. When you came into the town hall in Lonetree, I couldn't believe my eyes. I wondered if you were a fantasy I dreamed up. I thought of you so often, I couldn't be sure." His lips twisted in a wry smile. "I'm sorry for the things I said to you. You are nothing like Caroline or Abigail O'Conner. You have courage and strength." He chuckled. "And surprising talents. How do you know how to shoe horses? How do you know how to shoot? I thought about the distance you shot Rex Conway, and it surprised me. Most women can't hit a tree if they stood in front of it. How do you know all these things?"

Maryanne smiled. "Let me finish your horse, and we'll talk."

"Okay." He let her chin go and watched as she screwed the last few posts in. "After all this time and all the searching, who knew a slip on the ice in Boston would bring you back into my life."

Maryanne straightened. "Your horse is done."

He stared at her. "Okay. Is there somewhere we can talk?"

A bear of a man in a leather apron walked in. "Maryanne, you've got two more horses to shoe. Customers are waiting."

Maryanne nodded. "John, I would like you to meet Jackson Daniels." She turned to Jackson. "Jackson, this is my boss, John."

John paused. His bushy eyebrows drew together. "Jackson Daniels? The man you went to Wyoming Territory to save and left me buried in work for? The Jackson Daniels you can't live without? The Jackson Daniels who can do no wrong? The Jackson Daniels you talk about incessantly?" He inspected Jackson from head to toe.

Maryanne knew her face went red. "Yes. John,

please don't say any more."

John held his hand out and shook Jackson's. "I expect I will have to find a new shoer. Maryanne is a farrier's dream. I knew this day would come when she came looking for work. I've never seen anyone so good with horses." He shrugged. "Oh well. So be it. It is wonderful to meet you, at last, Mr. Daniels. Now maybe I can get some sleep. Maryanne cries at night because she misses you." When Jackson's eyebrow rose, he hurried to explain. "She sleeps in the spare room. It's safer." He glanced at Maryanne. "Why don't you take the afternoon off and go talk to your young man."

She didn't knew where to look. Maryanne stumbled around to the front of Jackson's horse and removed the pipe and chain. His horse whinnied and side-stepped. She caught his bridle and rubbed the front of his nose. "It's okay, boy," she whispered. The horse stood still and nuzzled her.

Jackson untied his horse and took the reins. He led the horse outside and mounted it. He held his arm down to Maryanne. "Let's see how the posts do."

She glanced back at John. "I can't. I have work to do. Besides, I'm all dirty." She indicated her leather apron. "My hair is a mess."

Jackson chuckled. "You're beautiful to me. I don't care what you have on or how your hair looks. It's you I want to hold."

"I smell like horses," she said.

Jackson laughed. "So do I most of the time. Come on."

She blushed again as she untied her apron. She wanted him to hold her, too. John took her apron, and

Maryanne allowed Jackson to pull her onto his lap.

"We must look a sight. You in your fancy clothes and me in my work dress with my hair in my eyes. What if I get your nice jacket dirty or get black on your shirt?"

Jackson shrugged. "I'll get another one. Clothes are replaceable. You're not, so quit thinking up excuses."

"Aren't you on your way to something? You're too dressed up to not be."

"I'm on my way back from Granny's lawyers. They went over her will following the funeral. I was heading home when Sparta slipped." He patted the horse's neck. His arms tightened around her waist as he pulled her against his chest. "I'm ready for my answers," he said. He turned his horse toward the city park.

She took a deep breath. "I left after the trial because I thought you blamed me for getting you arrested."

He shook his head. "No."

"Well, you would be right to. It was my fault and my mess. I sent a telegram to Miss Gwen when I read about the trial in the newspapers. One of the girls kept in contact with Sadie. Sadie went to Omaha after the shooting and started a new life. She found a place to live and bought herself new clothes. She changed her name so William and his friends wouldn't find her. She put an advertisement in the paper and works as a lady's companion. She's doing very well. The last thing she wanted to do was go back to Lonetree. I made her come with me because the judge needed to know what Rex, William, and the others did." She swallowed, remembering her fear. "Walking into the town hall was the hardest thing I ever did."

"Because you knew you could be hanged for murder?"

Maryanne shook her head. "No." She trembled in his arms. "Because you were there. I couldn't bear to see your contempt. You were there for something I did. I knew what you thought of Abigail. I couldn't bear to see you look at me the same way."

Jackson squeezed her to him. "You're nothing like Abigail O'Conner. She didn't care for anyone but herself. You traveled to Wyoming Territory to turn yourself in. You were very brave and very foolish."

Maryanne frowned. "What other question? Oh, the horses." She brushed her hair from her face and frowned at her dirty hands. "I hated being in the house with Daddy. He was mean and blamed me for everything. He yelled at me all the time and said I made him miserable. So, I started going to the stables. The men were nice, and our stable master, Mr. Todd, let me ride every day. I went more and more. For the first time in my life, I fit in. I helped the men with the horses and the chores. Soon, I shoed all Daddy's horses, and I liked it. The horses liked me, too. I could get them to calm down when no one else could. Mr. Todd taught me to shoot and to fight. I became the son he never had, and Daddy never knew about any of it."

"You don't cook or sew, but you shoe horses, fight, and shoot."

Maryanne nodded. "Correct."

"You haven't answered the most important question."

Maryanne gazed up at him. She loved the feel of Jackson's arms around her. She soaked in their security and warmth. The terror of the last few months disappeared when he held her close.

They stopped beside a park bench. The streets were filled with Christmas shoppers. A thin blanket of snow covered the ground. Carriages rolled by on the cobblestone roads. A train whistled in the distance. Jackson slid off the horse with Maryanne in his arms. He let her down with care until her feet touched the ground. He tilted her chin to his and stroked her cheek while he gazed deep into her eyes. "I love you with all my heart and soul. You are courageous, strong, beautiful, and everything I could ask for in a woman. Will you marry me, Maryanne Wagner? I cannot live without you."

Hope resurrected inside her like a phoenix rising from the ashes. "Yes! Oh yes!"

Then his mouth descended to hers. He slid his tongue between her lips and drank like a starving man. Maryanne's blood heated. She couldn't believe she was here with Jackson. She wrapped her arms around his neck and kissed him back with all the pent-up longing and loneliness of the last few months. The kiss turned carnal. Tongue mated with tongue. Hands stroked and caressed, igniting a fire between them neither could resist. Maryanne's knees turned to jelly. Liquid heat settled in her stomach. She slid her hands inside Jackson's jacket and stroked his back with the tips of her fingers. Jackson groaned into her mouth.

The sound of a throat clearing caused Jackson to lift his head. A police officer sat on his horse in front of them. "I have a few concerns about the public display of affection you two are engaged in."

Maryanne's face flushed. She glanced at Jackson.

"We will go somewhere more private, Officer," Jackson said.

"See you do," the officer said. "As for myself, I'm glad love still exists in the world. It's the children." He indicated a carriage filled with a handful of youngsters gaping from across the street. The officer touched his cap and nudged his horse into a walk.

Jackson mounted his horse and held his arm down to Maryanne. "Come to Granny's and meet my aunt and cousins. You will feel right at home. Aunt Clara can take you shopping for a dress tomorrow, and we can set a date to meet with the pastor."

Maryanne froze. "I'm not dressed to meet your family," she protested. Then a new thought struck. "I didn't know you had family in Boston."

"My mother died when I was five. Her sister, Aunt Clara, raised me. When I got older, I moved in with Granny. She paid for my medical education. She was a grand old lady, and I loved her." He stayed silent for a second. They turned left down the next street.

Maryanne's eyes widened. "Your Granny lived in Beacon Hill?"

Jackson's eyes clouded. "Yes. Granny was one of the grand dames of Boston. She didn't want my mother to marry Chet Daniels. He was a poor man with nothing to recommend him but a kind and honest heart. He worked hard, and he lived hard. As time went on, Granny came to see his value. They worked out their differences and became friends before my mother died. My dad couldn't bear the memories after her death and moved to Wylder to start a new life. After the incident with the O'Conner's and Caroline, I decided to move to Wylder, too. I wanted to start a new life and put my old one behind me. Dad knew what I needed. He helped me see the situation from a whole new perspective. I'm glad I went to Wylder when I did. My dad died four months after I moved there."

Maryanne's heart rose high in her throat when they stopped. She had no idea why she thought Jackson a regular man. Nothing about him was normal.

They stopped in front of a two-story granite structure with big paned windows and wooden shutters. Large trees stood in the front, shielding the house from the street. Jackson urged his horse into the drive and around the back. He led him toward a large stable and helped Maryanne to the ground.

She bit her lip. She had no idea her day would turn out like this when she woke. She smoothed the front of her worn blue calico dress and tucked her hair behind her ears. "Your family will think you're marrying a pauper and toss me out on my ear. They'll think I'm after you for your money."

"No, we will think you are the answer to our prayers. Welcome to the family, Maryanne Wagner."

Maryanne whirled around to find the owner of the voice, a tiny, elegant woman with dark brown hair and hazel eyes holding her arms open to her.

Jackson smiled. "Maryanne, meet Aunt Clara." He bent and whispered in her ear. "I talked about you, too."

Aunt Clara tugged into the warmest welcoming embrace she ever felt. When Maryanne stepped back, she realized Jackson was right. She'd come home.

Chapter Fourteen

They were married two weeks later at the little church on Newbury Street.

At a party the night before, Jackson introduced her to so many people they all became a blur.

Until a blonde woman with a sultry voice approached. "So, you're Maryanne."

Maryanne turned toward the voice. She knew without being told this was Caroline. "I am."

Caroline inspected her from the top of her head to the soles of her shoes. "Oh," she said and turned away as if Maryanne were unworthy of her attention.

"You are?" Maryanne asked.

Caroline stopped. "I'm sure you know. Jackson must have mentioned my name. I am Caroline Miller Carter. I married Senator Carter, but it didn't work out." She dismissed Maryanne with a shrug of her elegant shoulder.

"Jackson hasn't mentioned you at all." *Of late*, she added in her head. "I'm sorry your marriage didn't work out. Perhaps someone will meet your standards someday."

Maryanne moved away to find Aunt Clara. Caroline made her way over to Jackson. Maryanne discovered she didn't care. Jackson gazed across the room and caught her eye. He inclined his head toward the terrace. Whatever Caroline said to him, didn't make an impression. He frowned, answered, and walked away.

Caroline watched him go with a look of surprise.

Maryanne met Jackson on the terrace. He swung her into his arms and kissed her soundly. "I can't wait until tomorrow night. You shall be Mrs. Daniels, and I'll have you all to myself."

Maryanne couldn't wait either.

Aunt Clara became a dear friend. She arranged everything in a whirlwind of activity. Dressmakers created Maryanne's dress of white satin with a long slim skirt in the front and a ruffled bustle in the back. Rows of seed pearls adorned the bodice of her gown, and delicate lace dripped from her elbows and the bottom of her skirt. Maryanne held a tiny bouquet of white rosebuds and delicate baby's breath. Forget-me-nots peeked around the roses adding color. A maid pinned her hair in curls high on her head and threaded it with strings of pearls. Pearl jewelry bedecked her neck, ears, and wrist. A beautiful diamond engagement ring sparkled on her third finger.

Maryanne slipped her feet into her satin heels and allowed Aunt Clara to cover her hair with the delicate lace veil.

"Hurry, dear, or we'll be late. The carriage is at the front door. Jackson will desert his post and come looking for you if you don't appear with the first strains of the wedding march."

Maryanne laughed. He would, too. Jackson didn't let her wander very far since the day at the farrier. Maryanne slipped her long gloves on and followed Aunt Clara down the stairs.

Aunt Clara had twin boys, Rulon and Roy John.

The boys were ten years old and a couple of comedians. They made her laugh with their antics. Maryanne enjoyed their company and spent several evenings losing at chess with them. The boys were smart as whips and already at the top of their class. Jackson expected them to go to Harvard and get degrees. Maryanne knew whatever they did, they would be successful. They had a wonderful family to support them. The boys were already at the church. They'd left with Jackson.

Maryanne's carriage arrived at the church with five minutes to spare. She couldn't believe her wedding day had arrived at last. In a couple of hours, her deepest desire would be realized. She would be Jackson's wife. They planned a honeymoon traveling down the eastern seaboard. Then they planned to settle in Wylder, and Maryanne couldn't wait.

She stepped from the carriage and walked with Aunt Clara up the stone steps to the double doors of the church.

Maryanne entered the church with a smile on her face. She stopped inside the entry and waited for the music to begin. Rulon and Roy John gave her away. They were serious about their task and walked her down the aisle toward Jackson with solemn faces.

Many of Jackson's old acquaintances filled the church. Maryanne knew by the smile on his face that the wrongs of the past were healed.

A shot rang out, and everyone froze. The organ music stopped. The church fell quiet. Maryanne took a deep breath and did a quick sweep. Everyone was fine.

"Stop this farce!" The congregation turned toward the back of the church.

Maryanne froze. Her father was here! Terror gripped her chest. She squeezed the boys' hands. "Run to Uncle Jackson where you'll be safe."

They shook their heads. "It's our job to protect you. You're our auntie now."

Their words touched a place in her heart she didn't know existed. They were right. These boys were her family. She gazed at Aunt Clara and Jackson. They were all her family. Her heart filled with joy. She belonged to them, and they belonged to her. She would never be alone again.

Maryanne turned and faced her father. He held a gun in his hand and pointed it at her chest.

"You ruined my life," he said. "I had everything I ever wanted until you came along. You killed her. You killed my love."

Understanding flashed across her mind. "Mama died in childbirth. I was a baby, Daddy. I couldn't control what happened."

"You could." He stared at her. Maryanne realized with a start he believed what he said. "You should have died and let my Gladys live."

Jackson moved beside her and took her freezing hand in his. "Go to your mother, boys."

"We can help," one said.

"We aren't afraid," the other one said.

"I know, but I need someone to take care of your mother. I'll take care of Maryanne."

They nodded and disappeared behind him.

Maryanne's knees knocked together. Her hands shook. "Give me the gun, Daddy. You don't want to shoot anyone." She held her hand out.

He laughed. "I'm not giving you anything but a

bullet in your heart. You took everything and left me with nothing."

"You didn't want me, Daddy. I gave you everything I had, but it was never enough." Her heart twisted when she said the words.

"You gave me nothing. I asked you to marry William Smythe. William came from money. He had position and power. You could have had anything you wanted, but you rejected him. You took his money and shot his friend." He glared at Jackson. "You gave your virtue to this scoundrel and embarrassed me in front of my friends. You're no good. You deserve to hang for what you did." He glanced around at the silent audience. "Is it too much to ask for a daughter to bring honor to the family? To obey her papa's wishes?" He spit on her beautiful gown, "I won't allow you to take from me anymore. Today I'll do the taking." He waved the gun in her face.

Jackson tensed beside her. She put a hand on his arm. "It's okay."

"No, it's not," he answered.

"He won't hurt me." She gazed into her father's eyes and read pain, not murder. "What do you mean I took everything? What don't you have, Daddy?"

"My money. I don't have the money!" he yelled.

"Mr. Smythe took his loan back," Maryanne stated. She shook her head over his sorrowful condition. His money meant everything to him. She realized it when he wouldn't listen about William.

William. Anger rose in her chest. "William was a horrible man, Daddy. You know what he did. He should have gone to jail years ago. You should have listened when I told you what he did to me. William got what he deserved."

Phineas Wagner howled with displeasure. He raised his other hand as if to strike her. "Don't say any more, or you'll be sorry."

Maryanne didn't flinch. Her chin rose in challenge. For the first time, she recognized him as an old man with nothing to live for. Her father held no more power over her. She took a step toward him and took the revolver from his shaking hands and handed it to Jackson. Then she hugged her dad. After a moment, he hugged her back. It was as awkward as first hugs are.

Maryanne stepped back. "You're welcome to stay for my wedding, Daddy, but when it's over, go home. If I decide I forgive you for threatening me on the happiest day of my life, I'll come and visit. If not, have a happy life."

Maryanne turned her back on him. She wiped the tears from her eyes.

Branch Wylder stood by Jackson's side. He came from Wylder to attend their wedding leaving Deputy Wilson in charge. He took the revolver Jackson handed him and slipped it inside his jacket. With a slap on Jackson's shoulder, he resumed his seat.

Maryanne held her arms out for Rulon and Roy John to continue their escort to the altar. They left Phineas Wagner standing in the aisle and continued with the wedding.

Once the ceremony ended, Maryanne glanced around. Her daddy sat in the back of the church. He nodded his head as he got up and walked out of the church without a backward glance.

Jackson squeezed her hand. "How did you know he would back down when you challenged him?"

Maryanne shrugged. "I didn't. I pictured how I would feel if you were taken from me. I wouldn't be able to bear it. I'm quite sure I would go a little crazy, too."

****

Jackson swung her up in his arms and carried her from the church to their waiting carriage. Aunt Clara planned a reception in their honor at Granny's house in Beacon Hill. She served a rich luncheon accompanied by champagne to toast the couple's health. They cut the five-tiered wedding cake and fed each other a bite. It tasted like sawdust in Maryanne's mouth. All she could see, or feel, was Jackson. Maryanne changed into a pale pink traveling gown and stood on the second floor next to the railing. She tossed her bouquet to the laughing girls below.

Then they left. Jackson reserved a suite at the Parker House Hotel where they would spend their first night together.

Maryanne ran her fingers over the glossy polished furniture in their elegant suite and wandered over to look out the window.

Jackson set their traveling cases on the wooden bench and turned toward her. His heated gaze traveled over her. "I have waited for this moment for months." Desire deepened his voice.

Maryanne nodded. Now they were alone, anxiety fluttered in her stomach. What if she did something wrong? What if he wasn't pleased? All her old insecurities rushed back along with the things William said to her. She bit her lip and took a step away from Jackson.

He stilled for a moment. With a welcoming smile,

he held his arms out to the side like a scarecrow and waited.

"What are you doing?" she asked. She smiled at his pose.

"Waiting for you to have your way with me," Jackson answered. He grinned. "I'm all yours. Do what you will."

She looked confused. "I don't understand. Don't you want to—"

"Very much," he answered. "But you're frightened. I know what you went through with William. I will never force you to do anything against your will. I won't rush you, Sweetheart. I love you. Your happiness is important to me. We can do as much or as little as you want."

She looked at the sincerity in his eyes and realized he embodied everything her heart desired. He created security, happiness, and love by being there with her. With a cry, she threw herself into his arms and kissed him with all the passion she possessed. He responded in a heartbeat, caressing, and stroking her until she cried out for his possession. They melded together in the darkness, becoming one in heart and body. Jackson filled every hole in her heart and soothed the wounds in her soul. He possessed, fulfilled, and satisfied her every desire until they fell over the edge together in blissful rapture, wrapped in each other's arms. When the last tremor of their lovemaking faded, Maryanne snuggled closer to Jackson.

"Thank you for taking a chance on me. You could have tossed me out on the street when you found me in your stall, but you didn't. You swore off rescuing ladies in distress, but I'm so glad you made room for one more."

Jackson smirked. "But you weren't a lady. You were a skinny boy with the most fascinating backside." He gave her an evil grin. "If I buy you a pair of men's trousers, would you wear them for me? In private, of course. I like looking at your back view when you wear them."

Maryanne laughed. "I would wear them every day if I could." She laughed. "If I'd known what waited for me in Wylder, I would have put on a pair and come months earlier."

Jackson tucked her head beneath his chin. She was nothing like the other women he had known. She was unpredictable, outspoken, and prone to trouble. She would take his well-ordered life and turn it upside down. He smiled. He couldn't wait to spend the rest of his life finding out what other surprises she had in store. One thing was for sure. Life wouldn't be boring.

A word about the author…

I have been married to my best friend for thirty-nine years. I enjoy knitting, crocheting, and quilting. My favorite flower is the rose, and my favorite dessert is lemon meringue pie.

I have two large dogs who keep me company while I plot. I don't know what I would do without them. I like to throw story ideas at my family when I write myself into a corner. They have been my greatest support and I appreciate each one of them for listening and throwing ideas back at me.

Thank you for purchasing
this publication of The Wild Rose Press, Inc.

For questions or more information
contact us at
info@thewildrosepress.com.

The Wild Rose Press, Inc.
www.thewildrosepress.com